Danger! Dinky Diplodocus

Written and Illustrated by

Scott E. Sutton

Action Publishing · Los Angeles

ISBN 978-1-888045-62-8

Library of Congress Control Number: 2010942071
10 9 8 7 6 5 4 3 2 1

Action Publishing LLC
PO Box 391
Glendale, CA 91209

Visit us online at actionpublishing.com

TOP SECRET – SCIENCE LOG – DO NOT READ!

THIS IS VERY TOP SECRET
DO NOT READ THIS – KEEP OUT!
ESPECIALLY MY LITTLE SISTER

Science Log #2
by Benjamin Banjo Montgomery
Paleontologist-in-Training
Photos by Lee Wong
Artwork by Banjo

Subject – We have a time tunnel in my dog's doggie door that goes back to the age of DINOSAURS and two weeks ago we went through it and almost got eaten by a family of T-Rexes. Do ... not ... laugh, it is true and it is awesome.

What happened – On Friday, two weeks ago at 4:00 exactly our secret Science Team – that is me, Banjo, my best friend Lee Wong, and my dog Dino – short for Dinosaur Dog – crawled through Dino's doggie door, which just happens to be the entrance of a TIME TUNNEL going back to dinosaur times.

What we saw – When we got there we saw lots of dinosaurs, like a giant herd of huge three horned Triceratops and some ostrich-looking dinosaurs with feathers and some duck-billed dinosaurs, too. Everything was cool until we tried to get back to the time tunnel entrance and get back home.

We ran into a mom and dad T-Rex. They were huge! We tried to sneak around them and we almost made it except I stepped on a stick – which was DUMB – and we woke up not one, but THREE T-Rex babies. These BABIES were SIX FEET TALL!

They chased us and we almost escaped but then they trapped us on some tall rocks. So we shot them in the nose with our slingshots, which was REALLY DUMB. The big parent T-Rexes got super mad and came charging after us. I THOUGHT WE WERE DEAD FOR SURE!

The dad T-Rex was just about to eat us alive when ... you will never believe this, but I swear it is true ... we were rescued by this ALIEN floating robot guy named ... Arbee. He picked us up and carried us to his big round silver UFO starship that he could disguise as a clump of rocks and trees.

He says that he and his assistant Zinzu are from some planet called 'Izikzah'. It is 100 light years from Earth.

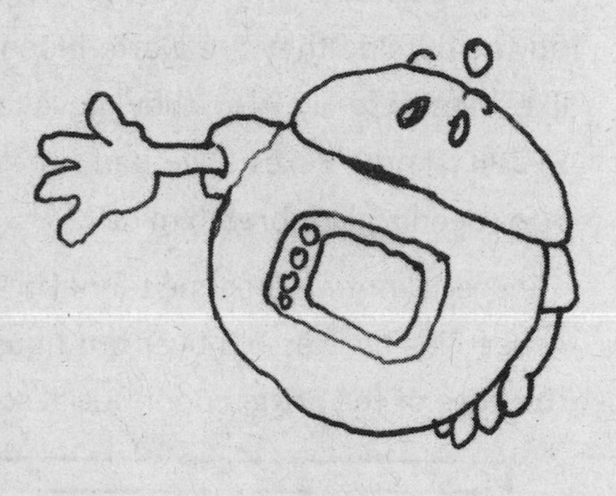

His people are a civilization of librarians and they have these cool starships that can travel back in time because they are studying the ancient histories of planets in this part of the galaxy. That includes Earth, too.

They collect all this knowledge and put it into their giant library so people from planets all over can come to Izikzah and study it. That is right I said ... people ... from ... other ... planets. There is life out there, folks.

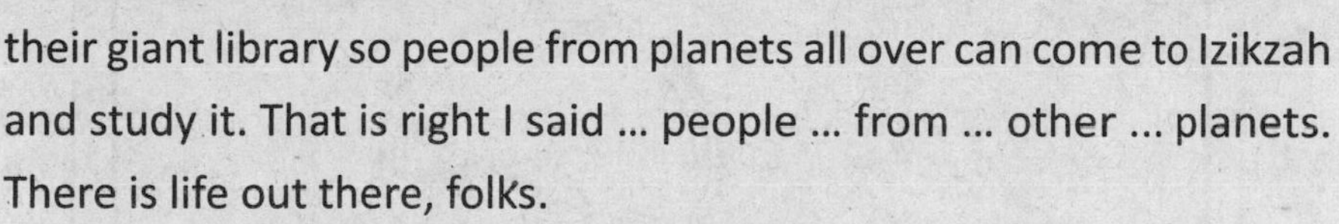

Me, Lee and Dino figured out that this Arbee guy was a good alien, not an evil man eating monster alien like you see in the Hollywood movies. So we made a peace treaty and became friends.

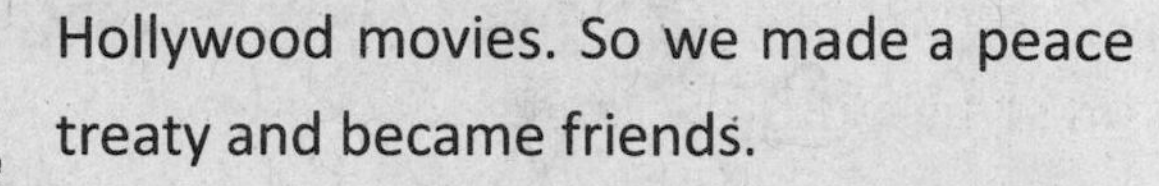

Plus, he promised not to take over the world or make us prisoners and eat us like moo-moo cows. He said his people did not have any use for Earth anyway.

He can also read Dino's thoughts and can talk to him, which is totally freaky!

Arbee took us out on a tour in one of his little shuttle craft to look around and we learned lots of stuff about dinosaurs.

We learned that even though dinosaurs look like lizards or birds on the outside they are warm-blooded, and they are all different, like animals today. Also, they move fast and they are definitely NOT STUPID. And T-Rexes have bad breath like you would not believe! They need a giant breath mint.

Special note – The time tunnel in Dino's doggie door forms when Arbee flies his starship over our house. It is because my dad made the edge of the doggie door out of some weird metal.

I replaced part of the doggie door edge with a fake piece so that the time tunnel would not form unless I wanted it to, because it forms every day from 4:00 to 4:30

That way Dino will not go through and get lost. And the last thing I need is for my little sister to crawl through the tunnel and get eaten.

She may be a little brat, but still, she is my sister. Plus my mom would get really mad and it would be totally hard to explain.

Very special note – Lee figured out that for every day that goes by in the past, only one minute goes by in the present.

Very special important note – The reason we cannot tell anybody about our discovery is because when we try to bring back stuff from the past it DISAPPEARS. Even photographs and videotapes come back BLANK.

Arbee said it is because you cannot take things out of the time they belong in. Anyway, if we told someone about this without proof they would say we were CRAZY and put us in JAIL or worse, send us to the PRINCIPAL'S OFFICE! WE would be grounded ... FOREVER.

Arbee said we could see him again in two weeks and it has been two weeks now so me and Lee and Dino are going back today after school.

Hopefully the locator coin that Arbee gave us last time will work. I would hate to get lost back there and get eaten alive because that would hurt ... really bad.

End of Science Log #2
Benjamin Montgomery

Chapter One
SWEET DREAMS

"LET GO OF IT! LET GO OF IT!" screamed five-year-old Cassie Montgomery, who was so angry she was almost in tears.

"GIMME IT, KID!" yelled a mean-looking dark-haired boy who was almost twice Cassie's size. "Hand ... it ... over ... NOW!"

"NO! IT'S MINE, DO YOU HEAR? NOT YOURS ... LET GO OF IT ... NOW!" she screamed back and stamped her feet.

Just then Cassie's older brother Banjo came walking around the corner with his best friend Lee Wong on their way home from school.

As soon as they saw what was going on, the two boys ran toward the Montgomery's front yard where the dark-haired boy was trying to steal a squirt gun from Cassie.

"HEY, NELSON!" yelled Banjo. "LEAVE MY LITTLE SISTER ALONE!"

The dark-haired boy was surprised and let go of Cassie's squirt gun. "Uh oh ... keep your squirt gun kid!" he said and started running fast across the front yard, away from Banjo and Lee.

As he was trying to escape he took a short cut across the Montgomery's driveway in front of their garage door.

But before he could get away there was a loud – CRASH!

The garage door exploded into splinters. Pieces of wood went flying everywhere.

Standing there where the garage door used to be was a very large and very angry meat-eating dinosaur that was over twenty-five feet long and ten feet tall.

The dinosaur spotted Nelson and instantly went after him.

Nelson screamed and tried to get away, but it was no use. The dinosaur's jaws grabbed him by the back of his shirt and lifted him off the ground, like a giant bird catching a helpless worm. Nelson's eyes were as big as saucers as the beast, growling angrily, swung the boy around by his shirt.

Cassie was screaming as loud as she could and jumping up and down.

Dino, the Montgomery's big Chow Chow dog, had run out and was barking wildly at the dinosaur, trying to bite its tail.

SCOTT E. SUTTON '02

"Oh, NO!" yelled Banjo. "A dinosaur found a way through the time tunnel. That's totally impossible. How could this happen?"

"AAAAA! My mom is going to be so mad that we brought a dinosaur home!" screamed Lee as he dropped his books and covered his eyes. "This can't BEEE!"

"BANJO!" screamed Nelson, still hanging from the dinosaur's long sharp teeth. "YOU GOT TO HELP ME ... PLEASE! CALL IT OFF ... HELP ME, BANJOOO ... BANJOOO ..."

"Banjo, Banjo ... come on, Banjo ... Banjo, wake up!"

"Huh? What?" grumbled Banjo, as he woke up suddenly. "Huh? Oh!" Banjo shook his head.

"Wake up, sleepy head. You fell asleep," said Lee, who was standing next to Banjo's bed.

"I had the weirdest dream ever just now," moaned Banjo, rubbing his eyes. Banjo told Lee about the dinosaur that came through the time tunnel and tried to eat Nelson Baxter, a friend of theirs from school.

"Have you been eating peanut butter and chocolate doughnuts again?" asked Lee, shaking his head. "Admit it."

"I like chocolate doughnuts and peanut butter," replied Banjo. "They are like, the perfect food."

"Yeah, but you always get those freaky dreams when you eat that garbage," added Lee. "That stuff is bad for you."

“Yeah, yeah, I know,” grumbled Banjo, as he ran his hands through his messy bright red hair.

“Well, no dinosaur is getting through the time tunnel as long as we have this,” Lee said smiling as he held up a strip of metal.

It was part of the edge of Dino’s doggie door. When it was not in place, the time tunnel would not form. The time tunnel, going back to the age of dinosaurs, appeared every day between 4:00 and 4:30 in the afternoon. Dino had almost gotten lost and eaten many times when he went through it alone.

If Cassie Montgomery found out about it, or worse, if she happened to crawl through it, well, Banjo did not even want to think about what could happen. Luckily, the garage was off limits to her, but they could not take any chances. Cassie was always sticking her nose into Banjo’s business.

Banjo looked at the clock next to his bed. “3:45! Oh, man! We have got to get ready!” he exclaimed.

“No kidding, hurry up,” replied Lee. “We only have fifteen minutes until we have to go. Arbee is probably waiting for us.”

The boys quickly checked out all their supplies and packed them carefully into their backpacks.

“I am still taking my slingshot,” said Lee, holding the weapon in his hands.

“Yeah, me, too,” sighed Banjo. “Even though they are

totally useless, especially against a Tyrannosaurus Rex, it just makes them really mad ... really, really mad."

"Not even a TANK would stop one of those things," said Lee. He remembered back two weeks earlier when they were hunted down and nearly eaten by a family of T-Rexes. The thought made him shiver.

"Arbee said he would land his starship in a safer place this time. We shouldn't have any problem on the other side of the time tunnel," said Banjo.

Banjo carefully stuffed the special coin that their alien friend had given them into his pocket. It was some sort of alien locater Arbee gave the boys so he could find them when they came through the tunnel.

"I don't think anyplace back there is safe," mumbled Lee. "Just hope he finds us quick with that coin thing he gave you. Whatever you do, do not LOSE it!" Lee warned.

"I won't, I won't. It's safe in my pocket, I swear. See?" said Banjo. "Come on, let's get going."

The boys put on their backpacks and ran down the hallway through the kitchen to the garage, where the doggie door time tunnel waited to be turned on.

"Banjooo!" called Mrs. Montgomery.

"Yeah, Mom," replied Banjo.

"Make sure you guys are extra careful with those slingshots," she said. "You could hurt somebody with those, so don't you dare shoot those things at anybody or any animals.

Do you understand?"

"We are always careful," replied Banjo. "We don't want to go to jail, you know."

"I know," she said, "but those things just make me nervous, that's all. Dinner will be a little late, like around 6:30, okay? Dad's bringing home some Mexican food. I ordered tacos for you."

"Okay, tacos at 6:30, got it," said Banjo. "Bye!"

"I swear, moms have eyes in the backs of their heads," whispered Lee as they entered the garage.

"Mom radar," laughed Banjo, "or mom-dar, nothing can escape it. I think moms can read minds too. You know, maybe moms are really ... aliens."

Dino, Banjo's dog was already there, happily wagging his puffy Chow Chow tail. "It's about time you guys got here," he thought. Somehow he knew it was time to go and he was ready.

Banjo put Dino's leash on him and clipped it to a belt loop on his camouflage pants. He then bent down to Dino's doggie door, unscrewed the fake piece of trim that he had made and started to carefully screw on the real piece so that the time tunnel would form.

"Eight minutes to go," whispered Lee.

"Yep," whispered Banjo.

"Don't you think you guys are a little old to be playing

army?" said a girl's voice that came from the doorway to the kitchen from the garage.

"Oh, no!" whispered Lee. "It's that sister of yours, Cassie!"

"We are not playing army," replied Banjo, while still fixing the dog door. "We are ... uh ... going hiking."

"Oh. Well, those camouflage clothes you two are wearing make you look like you're playing army to me. What are you doing to Dino's doggie door?" she asked.

"I am just tightening the screws," answered Banjo, trying to be cool.

"Five minutes," whispered Lee to Banjo.

"Why?" asked Cassie, her hands on her hips.

"So the edge of the doggie door doesn't fall on Dino's head, okay?" replied Banjo. "It might hurt him."

"Rrrr, woof!" Dino barked at Banjo's sister. He did not like Cassie Montgomery much. She used to always pull his tail and ears when he was a puppy. Dogs, especially Chow Chows, hate that.

"Quiet, you stupid dog!" said Cassie. "I am speaking to Banjo not you."

"If you were not part of this family, I would chase you like a rabbit," thought Dino.

"Don't yell at Dino," said Banjo.

"Humph! Are you sure you know what you're doing with that dog door?" she asked. "It looks very hard. Maybe you should tell Dad and let him fix it."

"Yes, I do know what I am doing and no, dad doesn't need to fix it. I can do it myself," said Banjo, starting to lose his patience. "Cassie, you're not supposed to be in the garage. Dad's orders," added Banjo. "Hah! That'll get rid of her," he thought.

"Hah! I am not IN the garage, I am IN the kitchen doorway, so THERE! NYAH! NYAH! NYAH!" she yelled, as she did her "I am better than you" dance.

"That kid is a pest," thought Dino "Can't we trade her for a cat or a squirrel? Squirrels are good."

"Two minutes!" whispered Lee desperately. "We may have to cancel the mission," he added. Lee put his hand on the doorknob, ready to open the door in case Cassie wouldn't leave. Opening the door kept the time tunnel from forming.

Banjo was trying to think what to do ...

"Cassie, close the door to the garage and leave your brother alone, please," said Mrs. Montgomery, from the kitchen.

"Phew! Saved by Mom," thought Banjo.

"Humph ... OKAY, Mom." Cassie replied. "You might be off the hook this time Benjamin Montgomery, but I am telling Dad you did something to Dino's doggie door, so ... there!"

“Fine with me,” replied Banjo, shrugging his shoulders and still trying to keep cool.

“Cassie, get out of here,” thought Lee, “there are only 45 seconds to go!”

“CASSIE!” called Mrs. Montgomery. “NOW, please!”

SLAM – Cassie closed the kitchen door and was gone. At just about the same instant – FLASH, POOF– The time tunnel formed and blew open the flap on the doggie door.

“Let’s go before she comes back,” said Lee.

“We ... are ... out of here,” replied Banjo.

“Finally!” thought Dino. “I thought she would never leave. Maybe we could trade her for another dog. Dogs are so much nicer than people and so much better looking, too.”

Dino and the boys dove into the time tunnel like rabbits down a hole and disappeared somewhere into Earth’s far distant past.

Chapter Two
FISH FOOD

"Oof, watch it, Banjo!" said Lee. The boys stumbled over each other and onto the ground trying to get out of the time tunnel.

"Sorry," Banjo replied. "I wasn't paying attention." Banjo was too busy looking around at the strange new surroundings that they were in.

Lee stood up looking at his hands. "Check this out, the dirt is reddish-orange."

"Yeah," replied Banjo, picking up a handful and letting it slip through his fingers. "Looks like Arizona dirt to me. The weather is different, too. It's warm and dry."

"It's much better than the hot and humid weather we ran into last time," added Lee. "The plants look different, too. Check out all these weird little ferns all over the place."

“You know,” explained Banjo “this place is rather pleasant, actually. I think I shall build a hotel and resort here,” he said in a joking voice, waving his hand in the air. “I think I will call it ... BANJOLAND! Yes, it is perfect. I will make millions of dollars, I tell you, millions!”

Lee laughed. “I can see the TV commercial now ‘Come to BANJOLAND! Get a sun tan and then be the first person on your block to be eaten by a psycho meat-eating dinosaur of your choice! They come in a wide selection of colors, shapes and sizes’.”

Both boys laughed.

Dino barked at the sky as a huge ten inch long dragonfly flew slowly above them. “Look, a giant bug. I saw it first,” he thought. “I say we chase it!”

“Lee,” whispered Banjo, “look at the size of that thing. It’s a super-sized dragonfly!”

Just then, from a nearby forest of giant ferns and palm trees flew two long tailed flying creatures. They were about the size of big crows and screeched like parrots. In an instant they had grabbed the large insect out of the sky, tore it in half and flown off into another forest of tall ferns and palm trees to devour it.

Dino barked like crazy. “Birds ... they have birds here,” he thought, “and they stole my bug!”

“Whoa!” exclaimed Lee. “What the heck were those things? They were not Pteranodons, were they?”

"Rhamphorhynchus," replied Banjo, rubbing his chin.

"Rhampho ... what?" asked Lee.

"RAM – fo – RINK – us," pronounced Banjo. "I could tell from the long tail with the diamond shaped fin on the end. I know how far back in time we are now, Lee."

"You do? So, how far back are we?" asked Lee.

"Those flying dinosaurs, the Rhamphorhynchus, lived about one hundred-forty-five million years ago," Banjo replied, looking through his dinosaur book that he had loaded onto a small hand-held computer. He pointed to one of the pages. "See?"

"Holy cows!" whispered Lee. "We are waaaay back. Huh?"

"Yep. Come on, let's look around some while we are waiting for Arbee," said Banjo, as he pulled Dino off into the direction of a small stream.

"Hey, wait up!" yelled Lee, running after Banjo. "We can't just go running around here like it's your backyard, you know. There are dinosaurs all over the place! What if we run into a pack of T-Rexes like we did last time?"

"Don't worry," Banjo called back. "Arbee said it would be safe. Besides, there are no T-Rexes this far back in time. Come on, let's go."

"Safe? There is no SAFE here," mumbled Lee to himself. "Nothing is safe around here. My mom would freak if I get eaten!"

Lee caught up to Banjo and Dino, who were walking through the thick ferns along the edge of the stream. The water was crystal clear and Dino ran to the water to lap up a nice drink.

"Mmmm," he thought, "tasty water." Dino loved to play in streams and walking through the mud. "Ahhh, the feeling of wet mud squishing through my doggie toes," he thought. "To bad there isn't a house around that I can walk through with my muddy feet or a white couch to jump on, that would make it a perfect day."

"You like water, huh, boy?" laughed Banjo, rubbing the top of Dino's head.

"As long as it's not a bath," thought Dino. "I love the mud and hate baths."

"My cat hates water," laughed Lee.

"Is that because you shot it too many times with a squirt gun?" asked Banjo, giggling.

"Nope," said Lee, "it's because one time she chased a skunk and it sprayed her so we had to give her about ten baths in two days. That cat stunk really bad! She probably thought the skunk was a black and white cat. Hah, Surprise!"

"Skunks are gross!" laughed Banjo. "Hey, check this out!" Banjo pointed to a lake over four hundred feet across, surrounded by round red boulders and a fern forest.

It looked like a postcard from a tropical island. The boys scurried over the smooth red rocks to the pool's edge.

"Oh, man," whispered Banjo. "Hey, Dino, don't go in there. That's deep."

Dino stopped about one foot past the water's edge. He sniffed the water as he looked into the clear green pool. "It doesn't look that deep," he thought. "Maybe there is stuff we can chase in here, like some fish or something."

Lee was standing on a big boulder overlooking the pool when he noticed something move under the surface of the lake. "Hey, Banjo get Dino out of there QUICK!" he yelled. "There is something huge moving under ..."

Before Lee had finished speaking Banjo yanked Dino's leash and pulled him out of the water.

At the same time Dino leaped backward just before a very large, light green fish creature shot to the surface and exploded from the water. Dino had scrambled to safety, but Banjo, trying to get Dino out, slid off a moss covered rock and fell – SPLASH – part way into the water.

"AAAAH!" screamed Banjo as he tried to get out of the water. But the boulders were too slippery and he kept falling back in. The giant fish creature grabbed Banjo by the shoe and tried to drag him back into the pool.

"LEEEE, get him OFF me! Let go of my SHOE, FISH!" Banjo screamed. He wildly pounded the creature's head with his fists. "OOF, OOF! Let me GO... STUPID ... FISH!"

Lee was stunned. He was trying to figure out what to do. He grabbed his slingshot and found a rock to shoot. But before Lee could fire the shot, Dino leaped into action.

The fish creature's long tail had come out of the water close to where Dino was at the edge of the pool. Dino charged in, bit the tail and started shaking it violently. The angry, growling Chow Chow began to drag the long, slimy fish out of the water, but it still would not let go of Banjo's foot. "I got you, you big fish. Let go of Banjo," he thought. "Ugh, you taste terrible. What have you been eating, rotten eggs?"

Lee jumped down, grabbed a big rock and threw it right at the creature's head – WHAP. The fish let go of Banjo's foot for just a second but it was enough time for Banjo to scramble away from the monster fish.

Dino was still trying to drag the fish out of the water. The creature was thrashing wildly, trying to bite him and get away. Water was flying everywhere.

"Dino, COME! COME HERE!" yelled Banjo.

But Dino was mad and would not let go. "Nobody messes with my family," he thought. "Nobody! I'll chew you like a dog toy, you stupid fish! Grrrrr!"

"DINO, LET GO! GET OUT OF THERE!" yelled Banjo. "Drop the FISH!"

"I'll shoot it!" yelled Lee. He grabbed his slingshot, loaded it but suddenly there was a loud – CRACK – it was the sound of breaking trees and branches and it came from the fern forest behind the pool.

"LOOK OUT!" yelled Lee. His voice was drowned out

SCOTT E. SUTTON

by a loud roar. The boys dove out of the way of a 30 foot long meat-eating dinosaur.

It charged in and grabbed the huge fish with its sharp teeth. The fish creature made a horrible croaking noise as the dinosaur turned and ran back into the nearby forest with the wiggling fish in its mouth.

"Arf, arf, arf!" barked Dino wildly. He started to chase after the dinosaur thief. "That's MY FISH. I caught it, you bird-lizard!" he thought. "COME BACK HERE!"

"Oh no you DON'T!" yelled Banjo. He grabbed Dino's leash before he could take off after the dinosaur and the fish creature. "Dino, you STAY, you crazy Chow Chow dog!"

"Aw, come on! That big bird-lizard stole my fish," he thought. "I hate those bird-lizard things. Who invented those things anyway? Probably the same guy who invented cats."

"You know, you really should not be feeding these creatures. It is not like you are feeding pigeons or ducks or something," said a British-sounding voice from behind the boys.

"AAAAHH!" the surprised boys screamed and dove for cover behind some large boulders.

Chapter Three
LIGHT SHOWERS AND BUG SHUTTLES

"Oh man Arbee, you almost gave me a heart attack!" said Lee.

"Woo, woo, woof!" Dino barked, as he ran up to greet his friend Arbee. The red and yellow round shaped alien floated to Dino and patted him on his head.

"Hi, Arbee!" thought Dino. "Good to see you. Did you see that fish I caught? It was as big as a car!"

"Well, well," said Arbee happily. "It is good to see you, my fuzzy little friend. Yes, I saw the fish you caught. Well done! Would you like a biscuit?"

"Woof!" Dino replied, sitting up on his hind legs with his tongue hanging out. Arbee pulled out a big dog biscuit and tossed it to Dino. Dino ate it like he had not eaten in three weeks. Dino always ate everything like he had not eaten in three weeks. "Yum, your biscuits are the best!" he thought, "They are like steak burgers."

"I am glad you like them, Dino, old boy," replied Arbee. "Now losing that fish does not seem so bad, eh?"

"Yeah, it tasted terrible," thought Dino, "and only dumb cats eat fish anyway."

"Sorry to scare you, boys," said Arbee as he floated over to Lee and Banjo. "What were you doing with that fish? They are very dangerous creatures, you know. They drag their prey down under water to drown it and then eat it. They eat almost anything. You really should not play with them."

"I know, I know," said Banjo, who was pulling fish teeth out of his shoe and tossing them into the pool. "We were not playing with it, it attacked us."

"Then when Dino tried to drag it out of the water that, dinosaur – probably an Allosaurus – grabbed the fish and ran away. He probably thought he could get a free meal," Banjo said. "He can have it for all I care."

"I thought you said it was safe around here," said Lee. "At least, that's what Banjo said."

"Well, next to the entrance of the time tunnel it is. But you should not be wandering around like you are in your backyard at home. There is a very active food chain going on here. You can not just walk right into the middle of it and expect to be safe!" Arbee explained.

"See, Banjo, I told you not to go running around, but do

you listen to me? Noooo!" scolded Lee, "You have to be mister explorer guy and get eaten by a giant fish thing!"

"Yeah, I know," Banjo replied. "Lee sounds just like my little sister ... yabbity, yabbity, yabbity," he thought.

"Are you hurt, Banjo?" asked Arbee.

"No, it bit me on the sole of my shoe," replied Banjo, trying to wash the smelly slime off his hands.

"Banjo ... you totally smell like an old fish!" laughed Lee.

"Grrrr, I am the fish monster!" Banjo joked, sticking his hands up in the air. "Let me hug you ... to death! Ha, haaa!"

"No way, get out of here, you wacko," laughed Lee as he ran away from Banjo.

"Come along, you three. We will go back to the ship and get you cleaned up and dried off," suggested Arbee. "You all could use it."

They set out back toward the time tunnel and Arbee's starship.

"My dad would love to fish here," said Banjo.

"Yeah, it's the only place where you get eaten by what you catch," said Lee. "If my mom knew what I was doing ..."

"Hey, Arbee," said Banjo, "I figured out by the dinosaurs that we saw that we have got to be at least one hundred forty-five million years or more in the past. Am I right?"

"Close, my boy, close," replied Arbee. "We are one hundred forty-six million years back in time."

"So the dinosaur that grabbed that big fish must have been an Allosaurus, right?" added Banjo.

"Correct," said Arbee. "That creature you saw was what your paleontologists call 'Allosaurus'. It is the largest meat-eating dinosaur in this time period. It is similar to the Tyrannosaurus Rex, but it is smaller and has larger arms."

"Wow!" sighed Banjo. "I wonder why it didn't eat us."

"Yeah," added Lee, "he could have just grabbed us, no problem. We were just lucky, I guess."

"The dinosaur, more than likely, thought you three were just scavengers of some kind," said Arbee. "Fish is probably a rare treat to Allosaurus, so it stole the meal and ran off. They eat almost anything they can, dead or alive."

As they walked through the bright green fern covering the red ground they heard what seemed to be a strange, animal call far off in the distance. The boys stopped.

Dino sniffed the air and whined quietly, trying to use his dog senses to identify what had made the noise. "Whatever that is, it sounds big," he thought.

"What was that noise?" whispered Lee. "Do you hear it, way over that way somewhere?"

Arbee looked off to the east. After a short silence there came another of the strange sounds.

"Sounds spooky, like elephants in a cave ... big elephants," said Banjo quietly.

"Those sounds you are hearing," said Arbee, "belong to the next type of dinosaur that we will be studying."

"What are they?" asked Banjo.

"That is a herd of Diplodocus," Arbee replied. "It is pronounced – di – PLOD – o – cus."

"Diplodocus ... really?" exclaimed Banjo. "Awesome!"

"Yes," answered Arbee, "they were some of the largest animals that ever lived on your planet."

"Those are plant-eaters," mumbled Lee as he looked "Diplodocus" up on the computerized dinosaur book they brought. "That's good, but, where there are plant-eaters, there are meat-eaters hanging around to eat them and that's bad," he added, shaking his head. "This just never seems to get any better."

SCOTT E.
SUTTON

The group finally reached the time tunnel entrance and behind it was what looked like a large fern tree forest. Arbee floated up and put a finger on his right wrist. A door opened at the edge of the forest, in mid-air.

"Wow!" said Banjo. He picked up a small pebble and tossed it at the forest – THUD – it bounced off something metal and fell to the ground.

"As I explained to you on your last trip, this is a screen made by the starship's computers that make it look like the surrounding forest," said Arbee. "That way, I can study these creatures in complete secrecy and so I do not upset them. They are very sensitive to changes in their territories. I do not want to scare them off."

"Great camouflage," said Lee, smiling. He liked being close to the starship and the time tunnel. It made him feel much safer and closer to home.

"I need one of these to keep my little sister out of my room," said Banjo. Lee laughed. "I need a computer camouflage screen."

"Come this way, my friends," said Arbee as he guided the boys and Dino through the starship's doorway.

The inside of Arbee's starship was very clean and simple, not like space ships the boys had seen in the movies.

The hallway walls were coated with a hard, smooth, dark blue type plastic. The floor was dark blue, too, but it was covered with a strange hard rubber. It felt soft to the touch.

In the ceiling were warm yellow lights. It gave the ship a comfortable feeling.

Arbee took them to a room. In the middle of it was a round section of the floor that was raised about two feet high and was about ten feet across. Arbee pointed to it.

"Lee, Banjo, and Dino, climb up on the raised part of the floor, will you please?" asked Arbee.

The boys did as they were told. Dino sniffed the platform and then jumped onto it. "Hmmm! Seems okay," he thought. "It better not spray me with water or I am ... out ... of ... here."

"What is this?" asked Lee, a little nervous.

"It is like a shower but without water. It will clean you all up in just a few seconds," Arbee said cheerfully. He put his hand on the wall next to him. As he did, a computer panel appeared. He pushed some buttons and Dino and the boys found themselves covered in different, brightly colored lights.

"Hee, ha, ha, hee, oooh! Hey, this thing tickles!" laughed Banjo, squirming around.

"I don't think you're supposed to be moving around on this thing," said Lee. "I don't want it to blow us up. Hold still, Banjo!"

In just a few seconds the lights went off. Dino and the boys were dry and clean. Dino shook his fur out. This light shower made his hair and skin feel good and clean. It even got rid of a couple of fleas that had been hiding in his ears. The best part was that he got clean without being sprayed with a hose. He hated baths. "We really need one of these at our house," he thought.

"This is the coolest thing, ever!" exclaimed Lee. "No dirt, no wet, no smell, my mom would LOVE this thing. You could make a zillion dollars selling these things on Earth."

"No kidding," added Banjo. "I would take a shower more often if I had one of these babies."

"Wait a minute, we are not going to turn into mutants or monsters because of the light from this thing are we, Arbee?" asked Lee. "You know, like, grow a new eye or horns, something weird like that?"

"You watch too many 'Space Aliens Destroy the Earth' movies," laughed Banjo.

"No, no," laughed Arbee. "It is quite harmless and it will not turn you into a monster. It just cleans you up, that is all. Now then, let us get to the shuttle dock and track down the herd of Diplodocus."

They quickly made their way up to deck number five of the starship where Arbee kept his shuttle craft.

"We will take this one here," said Arbee, pointing to a small shuttle that looked like a big copper colored bug without any legs. "The craft we used last time is being repaired. But this one is much tougher."

"Shuttle craft two ready for departure," said a high, squeaky voice.

"Hi, Zinzu!" said Lee and Banjo.

"Woof!" barked Dino. "Hi, Zinzu!" he thought.

"Hello, Mr. Banjo, Mr. Lee and you, too, Dino. Nice to see you all again," said Zinzu, as he floated into the light. He was smaller than Arbee but he had eight eyes and eight arms in a circle around his body. He was the second in command of the starship.

"Thank you, Zinzu," said Arbee. "We are going be in the field for quite some time."

"Very well," replied Zinzu. "Call me if you need assistance."

Arbee led Dino and the boys on to the small craft. "You sit back here in the passenger section. You will be able to see very well through these windows. And we even put this bench down the middle so you can sit, as well."

"Thanks. Great," said Banjo, but the boys did not sit. They were too excited. They each stood by a window so they could see out.

Dino jumped up on the bench and looked out one of the windows, then out another. "Riding in these shuttle craft things is great," thought Dino. "It's really easy to see squirrels, except I have never seen any around here. They must be hiding."

"Sorry to disappoint you, Dino, but squirrels will not be around for millions of years yet," said Arbee. "Lee, Banjo ... I will be up this hallway in the control center and we will be able to talk to each other with the shuttle craft's radio."

"Okay," the boys replied, still staring out the shuttle's windows.

Arbee floated to the control center.

"Hello back there. Can you hear me all right?" asked Arbee, testing the radio.

"Yeah, just fine," answered Lee.

"Woof, woof," barked Dino.

"And Dino, too, excellent!" replied Arbee. "All right, prepare for takeoff in three seconds ... two ... one ..."

Chapter Four

IT'S NOT JUST A SLINGSHOT ANYMORE

The shuttle craft launched out of the starship and sped off to the east. The rich red ground passing below the shuttle was covered with palm trees and fern forests, giant red boulders and light green, crystal clear streams and lakes.

"This place looks like Mars or something," whispered Banjo, his nose pressed against a window. "Red dirt, red rocks everywhere."

"It looks like Arizona to me but it's definitely no place to go swimming," Lee mumbled. He was holding onto the side of the shuttle as tightly as he could. "Man, this thing goes so fast. Arbee drives like my mom."

Dino was next to him looking out the same window, whining. "What a place to hunt! Let's park this thing and get out. Maybe we can catch another fish!" he thought.

"Hold on tight back there," said Arbee.

It was already late afternoon in dinosaur time. "We are going to study what the Diplodocus herds do during the day and what they do during the nighttime as well," Arbee said.

As the shuttle craft flew on, the boys noticed the forest getting thicker. There were not only ferns and palms now, but also very tall trees, similar to redwoods with bright green leaves and reddish-brown trunks.

In a clearing among the trees the boys saw what looked like tree trunks but without any leaves.

"Weird trees," mumbled Lee, but he jumped back when he saw one of them move. "What are those things?"

"Diplodocus," yelled Banjo, "those are Diplodocus. Look at them, they are unbelievable!"

They could see over forty animals, some were on four legs and some were up on two hind legs reaching to the tops of the tallest trees and stripping whole branches of their leaves. The long-necked plant-eaters were gigantic.

"Those cow-lizards things are way too big to chase!" thought Dino. "What do they feed those things, anyway?"

"I can't believe I am seeing this," said Banjo. "Wait, I've got to get this stuff down." Banjo quickly grabbed his small computer from his backpack and began typing in the dinosaurs' colors so he would not forget them.

They were a blotchy dark brown color on their backs. Their underbellies were a light brownish-orange. A few of the bigger creatures had reddish-orange flaps of skin under their chins.

"These things are the biggest things, ever," said Lee. "If one of those things stepped on you, you'd be smooshed like a grape."

"Hey, Arbee," said Banjo, "the ones with the colored skin under their chins, are those males?"

"Yes," Arbee replied. "Those are the males. Hold on. We are going to land in a nearby clearing so we can get a closer look."

The shuttle craft dove straight toward the ground, coming to a quick stop just before crashing. They landed gently in a small clearing about five hundred feet from where the Diplodocus herd was feeding.

"Everybody out," commanded Arbee as he floated down the middle of the shuttle and out the back hatch.

Lee was first out of the shuttle after Arbee, glad to get his feet on solid ground after that landing. "Phew, you drive just like my mother, Arbee," mumbled Lee.

Banjo left the shuttle with Dino who was impatiently tugging at his leash to go explore. He was sniffing the ground to find something to chase, "I wonder if there are any rabbits around here?" He thought.

"Sorry, Dino," said Arbee, "both rabbits and squirrels are not living here yet. Now, boys, before we proceed I want to give you both something." In his hand he held a metal container filled with shiny metal spheres that were a little bigger than marbles. "Do you have your slingshots with you?"

"Well, yeah," replied Banjo, a little confused.

"Excellent, now take them out and bring them to me, please," Arbee said. "Quickly now, we do not have all day."

The boys did as Arbee requested but they were wondering what he was doing. Arbee set the container of silver marbles on the ground and took Banjo's slingshot.

"Alright," he continued, "pay very close attention. I know that you are children and are not allowed to have weapons in your time, which is fine. Without some sort of defense here in the past, however, you could find yourself in very serious trouble, as you have already experienced. I am sure you remember that family of Tyrannosaurus that tried to eat on your last trip."

"How could I forget THAT?" said Lee. "We were almost dinosaur snacks."

"Well, I developed a way for you two to defend yourselves using your slingshots if you find yourselves in a life-threatening situation," Arbee said.

Arbee took one of the silver marbles and loaded it into the slingshot's pouch. He located a small feathered dinosaur chasing an insect about fifty feet away.

He aimed and fired the marble at the dinosaur – WOOOSH – the marble flew at the running creature. As soon as it got within five feet of it – FLASH – there was a

SCOTT E. SUTTON

silent explosion of blue light.

The running dinosaur dropped to the ground like a rock in a cloud of red dust and feathers. It did not move.

"How did you do that?" thought Dino. "Can you catch squirrels with that thing?"

"Awesome," exclaimed Banjo.

"You killed it!" exclaimed Lee.

"Nonsense," replied Arbee. "I merely stunned the little fellow, you see? There is no sense killing things for no reason, you know."

"How long will it be asleep?" asked Lee.

"Once the animal is sleeping," said Arbee, "you have fifteen minutes to get away before it wakes up. There are no after effects at all and the creature wakes up fully alert and goes about its business as if nothing happened."

"Will it work on an Allosaurus or a Tyrannosaurus?" asked Banjo.

"It works on ANY life form," replied Arbee.

"And how close do you have to shoot the marble so that it works?" asked Lee

"You must get the marble within five feet of whatever it is you are shooting," said Arbee. "Now then, listen carefully, these are NOT toys! They are for self-defense only and you must give them back to me before you leave to go back to your time. Do you understand?"

"Yeah, and no shooting the dog with those things, because if you do I will bite you ... when I wake up," thought Dino.

"I will be very careful," answered Lee. "I swear."

"Can I try one?" asked Banjo, excitedly.

"You both may try one," said Arbee. "But I want your promise that you will not play around with these, Banjo."

"I promise," replied Banjo. "The last thing I want is to get killed with some alien weapon."

"Very well," said Arbee. "Lee, you go first. Load your weapon with one of the flash marbles."

"Okay," replied Lee. He picked up a flash marble and loaded it. "What should I shoot at?"

"Shoot at this," said Arbee, as he released an oval object into the air. The object flew up into the sky quickly, but not quickly enough – THWACK, SWOOSH, FLASH – the oval object dropped to the ground and disappeared.

"Excellent shooting, Lee!" exclaimed Arbee.

"Lucky shot," Banjo joked.

Lee smiled, "That wasn't luck. That was skill ... because I got slingshot skills."

"Grrrrrr," Dino growled a low warning, his lips curled up to show his sharp white teeth. "Something is coming," he thought, "and it smells like one of those giant bird- lizard things."

“I think something’s coming,” whispered Banjo. “Dino smells it.”

Suddenly, from bushes in front of them there came a low growl. “Errrrrr, hisssss,” and then they heard a – thud ... thud ... thud – like footsteps in the soft dirt. There was a pause and then – CRASH – a large brown creature leaped through the brush and into the clearing.

Banjo looked into its yellow eyes, saw its long sharp teeth and knew instantly what the creature was, “Oh rats,” he whispered. “It’s a big meat eater!”

Chapter Five
SO WHAT'S EATING YOU?

Arbee told the boys to stay quiet and still. Dino, however, was still barking and growling. Banjo did not even bother to try stopping Dino because he knew it would be a waste of time. Instead he turned to Lee.

"Hey, Lee," he whispered, "slide the can of flash marbles over here, quick!"

Lee nodded and did so very slowly, very quietly.

The dinosaur turned his head back and forth looking at Arbee, Dino and the boys. It walked over to the small feathered dinosaur that Arbee had knocked out, sniffed it. Then it pushed it with its snout, scooped it up in its mouth and devoured the helpless creature in a few bites. A piece of its tail that had not been eaten flopped onto the ground along with some feathers.

"Gross!" whispered Lee with a frown. "He swallowed

that thing whole. What a pig!"

"Arf, arf, arf!" Dino continued to bark at the beast, trying to scare it off.

Banjo took advantage of the delay. He reached down and grabbed a flash marble and loaded it while the dinosaur was eating.

The dinosaur finished its meal then turned to Arbee, Dino and the boys. It stared at them with an evil look in its yellow eyes. It lowered its head and without warning it charged, its deadly mouth wide open.

In a split second Banjo aimed and fired at the oncoming monster – THWACK, SWOOSH, FLASH!

"Got him," yelled Banjo.

"No, you DIDN'T, it's still coming. GET OUT OF THE WAY!" screamed Lee.

Dino was going to charge, but the boys grabbed him and leaped out of the way of the oncoming beast. Then – WHUMP – there was a ground-shaking thud and a cloud of thick red dust filled the air. When the dust had cleared some the boys got up. They saw the dinosaur had fallen about five feet short of where they were.

"Holy cows!" said Lee in a shaky voice.

"Phew!" Banjo sighed, wiping red dust from his face.

"Banjo, that was too close," said Lee. "Way too close!"

"Grrr, arf, arf!" said Dino, "I hate those things. Let me

bite it," he thought, "pesky bird-lizards!"

Arbee was still just floating there, hands on his hips, very calmly looking down at the now sleeping dinosaur.

"Well, good shot, Banjo, my boy," he said. "But you really should try to shoot these creatures before they charge, you know. It could get quite messy if one of them lands on top of you, quite messy, indeed."

The boys cautiously approached the sleeping beast. Its eyes were closed and it was breathing slowly.

Dino hung back cautiously, growling. "Are you crazy? I am not going near that thing," he thought. "People have no sense at all. They are dumber than cows sometimes."

"Do not worry, Dino," Arbee assured him. "It is asleep."

Banjo carefully looked over the animal. This was a meat-eater he had not seen before. He grabbed his computerized dinosaur book, scrolled through it quickly and studied a picture for a moment.

"Hmmm ... I think it's a Ceratosaurus. That's what it is, a Ceratosaurus," he announced finally.

"How do you know?" asked Lee.

"See that horn thing on its nose?" Banjo asked.

"Yeah," Lee replied, looking over Banjo's shoulder at the picture on the small computer screen. "Wow, that's what it is. Ceratosaurus, but it's not a very good picture."

"Hey, Arbee, if I touch it will it wake up?" asked Banjo.

"No," replied Arbee. "Now is a good time to get a close look at a live meat-eating dinosaur. You may never have a chance like this again. Go on, have a look. He will not bite, not for another thirteen minutes anyway."

Banjo walked over to the sleeping Ceratosaurus. It was a young one, about eighteen feet long. They were known to reach thirty feet long as adults. It was brown and dark orange.

Its coloring made it look like a Gila monster, the poisonous lizard that lives in present day Arizona and Northern Mexico. Its underbelly had the same coloring, only lighter. It also had some feathers in some places around its body.

Banjo leaned over and touched its skin. Lee did, too. It was very muscular, not skinny like in the dinosaur books.

"Its skin is like bumpy leather, but it's not like alligator skin at all. It's warm, too," said Banjo. "This is so awesome!"

"It's really thick and tough," added Lee, who tried to pinch and pull the dinosaur's skin. "I've never felt anything like this. It's not like lizard skin. More like bird skin or something,and check out these weird feathers along the top of his head and eyes."

"Yeah, some paleontologists thought meat-eaters were related to birds and that birds are really dinosaurs," added Banjo. "I think they were right."

The Ceratosaurus grunted and moved a leg.

"WHOA!" The boys and Dino jumped back, falling on the ground. Dino barked and tried to move further away, "You people are crazy, poking that thing like that! You are just asking for trouble."

"Are you sure he is sleeping?" whispered Lee in a panic.

"Positive," said Arbee. "He must be having a bad dream, or something."

"He IS a bad dream!" said Lee, brushing the red dust off his pants.

Banjo walked up to the head of the dinosaur and ran his hand over the flat horn on its nose. It was light reddish and looked like a cross between a horn and a fin, not like a cow horn. It was eight inches high.

"I wonder what that horn or fin thing is for," mumbled Banjo.

"I do not know," said Arbee.

Banjo looked into the dinosaur's mouth. "Well, it has a pretty long tongue and ... phew ... really bad breath. Oh, man!" Banjo stepped back, grabbing his nose. "Why does their breath always stink so bad?"

"From the meat they eat," replied Arbee. "Many times the meat they eat is not very fresh. As a matter of fact, they do not just hunt other dinosaurs. They eat the bodies of dead ones as well, like vultures do."

"Look at these claws," whispered Lee, who was still worried that the dinosaur would wake up and eat him. "They are sharp!" He poked them with his fingers and jumped back.

"These creatures were designed to hunt, kill and tear bodies apart to eat," explained Arbee, "and they are quite good at it. Well, we cannot stay here any longer. When our friend here wakes up he will be very angry. And they usually travel in groups of two or more. Back aboard the shuttle craft at once! There is more to see."

Banjo ran his hand one more time across the Ceratosaur's face. "This thing is built like a tank. Humans wouldn't stand a chance in this time," he said to himself, "not ... a ... chance."

"Oh, great," thought Dino, "he is playing with it. That is stupid, stupid and more stupid. Come on, Banjo, let's go!"

"Come on, Banjo," called Lee. "That thing's about to wake up and I don't want to be here when it does."

The boys, Dino and Arbee hurried back aboard the shuttle, but not before the boys filled their pockets with as many metallic marbles as they could carry.

Arbee flew the shuttle to the sky and not a minute too soon. Within seconds after they left, the Ceratosaurus woke up. It scrambled to its feet, shook its head and went about the endless job of finding its next meal as if nothing had happened.

Arbee piloted the shuttle to another nearby clearing with a good view of the Diplodocus herd. They all got off the craft and carefully made their way to within one hundred

SCOTT E. SUTTON

feet of the herd.

Banjo was counting as fast as he could, "38, 39, 40, 41, 42 ... I count 42 Diplodocus," he said, "but I can't see them all."

"They look so much bigger up close." whispered Lee, "They make me feel extremely wimpy."

Dino did not know what to think. He sort of hung back with his ears down and his tail between his legs, ready to run if he had to. "Those things are too big to chase! Can we go now?" he thought. "Can't we find some rabbits or some cats, maybe?"

"Sorry, Dino," said Arbee. "There are no cats here either."

"Don't tell me," thought Dino. "They haven't been invented yet, right?"

Banjo looked at Arbee. He still could not get used to Arbee talking to Dino as if he were a person.

There were about eight babies in the middle of the herd. Even they were big. But the adults were just massive at eighty feet or more in length and weighing as much as twenty elephants.

"Look! Look at them move," pointed Arbee excitedly. "It is as if they are floating. It is astonishing that an animal this size could move so smoothly! Do you agree?"

"Yeah," the boys replied, as if in a trance. It was true the beasts moved effortlessly, almost without a sound. They reminded Lee of elephants, big elephants with long necks.

"ERRRRROOOOOFF," one of the larger Diplodocus let out a loud call that almost knocked the boys off their feet.

"Oh man, that is SO loud," laughed Banjo.

"What a noise!" said Lee, as he covered his ears.

Dino sniffed the air and whined loudly. He backed away, tugging on his leash. "Something's wrong," he thought, "that smell, that smell means trouble. We need to get out of here, quick." He whined again.

Arbee looked at Dino. He knew what he was thinking, but before he could act the Diplodocus herd stopped eating and looked behind them. They were becoming upset.

Some of the larger Diplodocuses were stamping the ground on the far side of the clearing, as if they were trying to scare something away. The calling and stamping from the rest of the herd was getting louder with each passing second.

"What's wrong?" yelled Banjo. "What are they doing?"

"Something is frightening them. Dino smells something coming," said Arbee. "We had better return to the shuttle craft at once. Hurry, follow me."

As they ran back to the shuttle, the ground began to shake so hard that the boys were knocked off their feet.

"EARTHQUAKE!" screamed Banjo.

"NO ... It's a STAMPEDE," screamed Lee. "THE DIPLODOCUS HERD IS STAMPEDING!"

Chapter Six
RUN FOR YOUR LIVES, BOYS!

The frightened Diplodocus herd was charging straight for the shuttle craft. The boys had gotten back to their feet and were running on the trembling ground as best they could. It was like a bad dream ... running and falling, running and falling. They were making very little progress towards the shuttle.

"I WILL START UP THE SHUTTLE WHILE YOU GET ON IT!" yelled Arbee. "WE DO NOT HAVE MUCH TIME, HURRY!"

Arbee went ahead. He had to get that shuttle craft out of the way of the panicky herd. If a creature the size of a full grown Diplodocus stepped on the shuttle it could cause an explosion that would kill everyone and everything for a mile around.

Arbee flew aboard through a top hatch and into the

pilot's control area. He pushed a button that opened the rear doors so the boys could get in. There were only seconds remaining before the herd would be on top of them.

He tried calling to the boys, but even inside the shuttle the noise was too loud. Then he remembered the locator coin he had given Banjo. He pressed a button on the computer. Yes! It showed the locator signal was inside the shuttle craft. That meant the boys must be safely aboard.

Waiting until the last possible instant, Arbee quickly punched some buttons on the shuttle's control computer. He sent the craft into the sky seconds before the leg of a huge Diplodocus, that was as thick as a tree trunk, slammed to the ground creating an explosion of dust and rocks. The shuttle was safe. But what Arbee had not seen was that the locator coin was aboard, but the boys were not!

"NO ARBEE, WAIT! COME BACK!" shouted both Lee and Banjo. "STOP! WE ARE NOT ABOARD YET!"

Just before the boys and Dino had gotten to the shuttle the huge leg of a Diplodocus crashed down and blocked their way, blowing so much dirt and rocks in their faces they could not see. They barely caught a quick glimpse of the shuttle craft flying away through the thick clouds of dust and the necks of the dinosaurs.

But they had no time to worry about that now. They were in big trouble. There was so much noise, dust and commotion they had to scream and use hand signals to talk to each other.

Lee motioned to Banjo to run in the direction of the herd. If they ran crossways they would be trampled to death for sure. Banjo held on tight to Dino's leash and they all took off running as fast as they could.

The boys put every ounce of energy they had into running and trying to avoid being crushed. They fell several times and narrowly missed getting stepped on by a crazed Diplodocus. They had to find cover and they had to find it now.

"That log THERE ... huff, huff, huff," yelled Lee.

"NO! They will step on it for sure ... huff, huff, huff," replied Banjo. "KEEP RUNNING!"

It was a good thing they did not stop, for as soon as the boys ran past the log it was smashed into a million bits by the giant feet of the charging herd.

The boys were tired and out of breath but did not dare slow down. The loud calls and screams of the Diplodocus herd were as horrifying as the stomping and crashing sound of their giant feet on the ground.

"We have got to find a tree, puff, puff ... a ...TREE!" yelled Banjo.

"OKAY!" screamed Lee, as he looked around wildly for a tree, any tree.

Suddenly a huge shadow came over them all ...

SCOTT E. SUTTON

"LOOK OUT!" screamed Lee. "We're going to get stomped ..."

THUD – A giant Diplodocus leg came down, nearly crushing them. They were all knocked to the ground and were blinded by the flying dirt and dust.

"GET UP, QUICK," yelled Banjo, "HERE COMES ANOTHER ONE!"

They quickly got to their feet and – WHAM – another leg came down, knocking the boys down again. They got up again and were finally able to get out of the way of the gigantic dinosaur, but more of the frightened creatures were right behind it.

Dino was running ahead of Banjo and pulling on his leash to get away. "Got to keep running," he thought. "Got to get out of this and into the trees or we are dead."

The boys and Dino ran for what must have been ten minutes. The herd was starting to slow down some, but they had no idea where they were or how far they had come, and the chance that they would get trampled to death was still a very real possibility.

"That tree ... get behind it," yelled Banjo, pointing to a small grove of tall trees on the edge of the clearing.

They ran behind a huge redwood tree and dove for cover.

"Hissss, grrrr!" Two, feather-covered meat-eating dinosaurs had already taken over the hiding place that the boys wanted.

The angry dinosaurs lowered their heads, showing their long, sharp teeth and raised the feathers on their heads, ready to defend their hideout. The boys screeched to a halt, almost running right onto the angry beasts.

"Arf, arf, arf!" Dino barked a warning, making the feathered dinosaurs back away. They had never seen an angry Chow Chow dog before.

"Rats! This is no good, KEEP RUNNING TO THE NEXT TREE," yelled Banjo, "Go, go, GO!"

It was not long before the boys found a tree with a thick trunk. They ran to the other side of the redwood and hid in some fern plants at the tree's base. They collapsed, exhausted, dripping wet with sweat, trying to catch their breath.

"Huff, huff ... man ... that was the craziest thing I have ever done ... EVER," said Lee.

The charging herd ran past them on the other side of their hiding place making loud roaring calls as they went. Lee covered his ears. Dino trembled and whined. Banjo, too tired to do either, just watched.

Many of the gigantic plant-eaters were over a hundred feet long, at least. Dust and rocks flew up and the ground continued rumbled as they ran buy. The dust made the boys cough and made their eyes sting. Dino shook his hair to get all the dirt and rocks off of him.

"I miss chasing the little squirrels back home," thought

Dino, "These things are just too big. I mean they are CRAZY big."

"I thought those things couldn't move fast," puffed Banjo.

"Think again," answered Lee. "Another paleontology theory bites the dust."

Finally the herd passed and disappeared into the redwood forest beyond. The boys could hear an occasional Diplodocus call in the distance.

"Oh, man!" sighed Banjo. "We are safe for now ... I think."

"Shhh!" said Lee. "Look!" He pointed at something on the Diplodocus trail. "No, we are definitely NOT safe."

The boys saw what had caused the Diplodocus herd to panic and stampede. Across the dusty path, passing by their hiding place were four ... five ... no, seven large Allosaurs.

If the boys had been up in the shuttle craft when the stampede began they would have seen the group of Allosaurs, who often hunted in packs like wolves, attempt to charge past the protection of the giant parent Diplodocus and kill one of the younger plant-eaters.

Once the animal was attacked and killed, the Allosaurs would have waited for the herd to move on before eating their prey. But the attack had failed and one of the pack had been trampled to death in the stampede.

So the Allosaurs were on the trail of the Diplodocus

herd again to try to kill one. A single Diplodocus, even a baby, would supply the meat-eaters with food for many days.

Dino had smelled the meat-eaters before the stampede. "They smell just like those Tyrannosaurus things," Dino thought, still trembling. "Those big bird-lizards are nothing but trouble."

The boys got a good look at the monsters as they passed. They were light copper-colored with dark copper diamond-shaped spots on their backs and sides. The diamond-shaped spots were outlined in a faded yellow color. They also had a few small patches of feathers on parts their body.

"They look like thirty-foot-long naked birds with weird markings," whispered Banjo. "Those things are as dangerous as a Tyrannosaursus Rex ... maybe worse."

Soon the Allosaurs disappeared quietly into the forest.

Lee let his breath out. "This place is so dangerous I can't even believe it!" said Lee. "So, now what do we do? It's getting dark and we have NO idea where we are or where Arbee is."

"Don't sweat it, Lee. I have the locator coin Arbee gave me, remember?" Banjo assured Lee.

"Phew, I forgot about that," said Lee. "Arbee will have us out of here in no time."

Banjo, smiling, reached into his pocket for the locator coin and found ... nothing.

Chapter Seven
PREHISTORIC BABY SITTERS

"Oh no … wait … this can't be!" said Banjo. "I can't find the locater coin! WHERE IS IT?"

"Shhh, quiet!" said Lee. "Keep your voice down and check your other pockets."

Banjo checked each of the pockets on his cargo pants. "Nothing," he sighed. Banjo wanted to cry. "I don't know where I dropped it. I had it right here!" He was so frustrated. "It was right in this pocket, I swear!"

"You probably dropped it on the shuttle," sighed Lee. "That's why Arbee took off without us. He saw on his computer that the coin was on board. So, he must have thought we were on board, too." Lee was unusually calm.

"When he finds out we are not on the shuttle he will come looking for us," he added. "I hope he comes soon. This place is like walking through five monster movies all at once."

"But how's he going to find us? I don't have the locator coin, remember?" whined Banjo, running his fingers through his thick red hair.

"Computer sensors," answered Lee. "He can find us with the starship's computer sensors, remember? I think that's how he found us the first time, when those Tyrannosaurs almost ate us."

"Oh, man ... I really blew it," said Banjo, closing his eyes and leaning back against the tree. "Really blew it big time. I am so stupid."

Lee wanted to agree, but he did not. What good would it do? They had to stay calm and work out of this carefully. Lee worked well under pressure. He remembered a line from a book his dad had once read and told him about. How did it go? The best test of a person was their ability to make things go right or something like that.

"Banjo, we can't act like little kids. We have to solve this problem and get out of this mess," Lee said quietly. "We can't panic."

Banjo stared into the forest and took some time to calm himself. "Okay, it's getting dark. Where's the best place for Arbee to find us?" he asked Lee finally.

"I think we need to go back to where we started," answered Lee. "We follow the Diplodocus tracks backward until we get to where Arbee left us."

"Okay, we go back to where we started then," replied

Banjo. "But we had better stay on red alert. At least now we have some way to defend ourselves," he added.

They each took out their slingshots and loaded them with the flash marbles that Arbee had given them.

The boys and Dino crawled out from their hiding place and slowly made their way back to the trail made by the stampeding Diplodocus herd and started the long walk back.

"At least we will be walking in the opposite direction of those Allosaurs," whispered Banjo.

Off in the distance they saw lightning flashes in the sky. It made them feel more alone than ever, and scared.

"Okay, it's like you said, we are on red alert," whispered Lee. They both tightened their grip on their slingshots as they marched down dusty path ... into the unknown.

Back aboard the shuttle, Arbee had problems of his own. He had been observing the Diplodocus herd, now five miles away from where they started to stampede. His computer sensors, radio and electronics were going on and off. "Hmmm, what is wrong now?" Arbee mumbled.

Arbee called the starship, "This is Arbee to Zinzu, come in Zinzu."

There was a hissing sound and then, "Zinzu to Arbee. I can barely hear you. Your ... signal is ... breaking up."

"I am having problems with the shuttle craft's computers here. Do you know what could be causing it?" asked Arbee

"There is some sort of electronic storm around Earth. The electric energy around the planet at this time period is still very unstable. That is what is affecting the computers," answered Zinzu

"Do you know how long it will be before the storm passes?" asked Arbee

"I estimate at least ten hours or more," said Zinzu

"Very well, I am returning to the starship immediately. I should be there in a few minutes," said Arbee.

"I will meet you in the shuttle dock. Zinzu out."

Arbee pushed some buttons on the controls and flew the shuttle craft away from the Diplodocus herd and back to the starship. "Banjo, Lee and Dino, we are having some electrical problems and I must return to the starship." He listened for a reply, but just heard a hissing and crackling noise on the radio.

"Sigh ... even this radio is not working properly," Arbee flew on. "Oh well ... I will have to explain it to them when we get back."

The boys and Dino had been walking for a while when they heard some strange Chirping sounds coming from the bushes by the trail.

"Shhh, what is that noise?" asked Lee as he and Banjo raised their slingshots and aimed them at the bushes.

"Errrrr," Dino growled. "Watch out, there are some animals in the bushes ... some kind of bird-lizards I think," he thought.

"I don't know but ..." Banjo was interrupted by two feathered meat-eaters, about four feet tall, that jumped into the clearing and charged the Science Team.

"SCREETCH," they cried out.

THWACK, THWACH – the boys fired their sling shots and – FLASH, FLASH – the bird dinosaurs crashed to the ground with a thud, raising a thick cloud of dust and feathers.

"We got them," said Banjo. "These flash marbles are awesome. We sure could have used these on our last trip."

"No kidding, I love these things," added Lee. "That was so close."

"SCREECH!" a third dinosaur leaped into the trail near Banjo. "AAAAAH!" he screamed.

It moved so fast that it almost grabbed Banjo. Neither he or Lee had reloaded their sling shots, but the creature did not see Dino standing near Banjo's feet.

"GRRRRR, ARF," Dino growled and attacked. He jumped up and grabbed the dinosaur by the skin of its belly. He shook it violently causing it to scream with pain. Dino slammed it to the ground on its back. The creature managed to break away from Dino's grip just for a second. That was just long enough for it to retreat screaming back into the forest.

"ARF, ARF ARF," barked Dino. "You didn't expect to get into a fight with a Chow Chow dog, did you … bird brain? Don't mess with me … I'm a dog … from the future!" thought Dino.

"Dude, this place is so nuts, I cannot believe that we are still alive," said Lee, whose hands were shaking from the excitement.

Yeah, we have Dino to thank for that," said Banjo. "Good boy, Dino. You are a good dog," he said as he hugged Dino and picked some feathers out of the dog's mouth.

Dino licked banjo on the face. "No problem, bird-lizards are no match for Chow Chows," he thought.

"Yeah, thanks Dino. Hey Banjo, let's get going before these … whatever they are ... wake up and try to eat us again," said Lee. "What the heck are these things, anyway?"

"I have NO idea. I have never seen anything like them in any dinosaur book ever," said Banjo. "Let's keep our slingshots loaded and ready," he added, "there may be more of those things out there."

"I am loaded and ready, right," answered Lee.

The boys and Dino continued up the trail and remained extremely alert. They had walked for nearly a half hour when they heard the moaning sound from some sort of animal.

It sounded like a Diplodocus call but much higher.

"EEERRRRFFF!" went the sound.

"What's that?" whispered Lee, stopping and aiming his slingshot at the noise. "I hope it's not more of those psycho bird things."

"Shhh, I don't think so. Dino isn't growling," said Banjo. He signaled to Lee to follow him.

The boys made their way to the far side of the Diplodocus trail that was two to three hundred feet across. They stopped, listening for the sound.

"ERRRUMFFF!" There it was again. Lee pointed to a thicket of big trees, vines and bushes. Dino whined. His ears were moving, trying to locate the source of the sound. He sniffed the air. "Well, the good news is, it's not a meat-eater," he thought.

"Shhh, Dino," whispered Banjo. "Come on, this way."

"Yeah, yeah, yeah, whatever," thought Dino. "I've got news for you, Banjo ... these lizard things can sniff us out, they don't need to hear us."

They all moved toward the sound again. As they got closer they heard a sort of whimpering, like a scared or hurt animal.

"Through here," whispered Lee, crawling carefully through some vines and bushes on his hands and knees. He came to a clearing and was met with a dinosaur face attached to a long snake-like neck or body.

"AAAAH!" screamed Lee. "GIANT SNAKE, GIANT

SNAKE, I HATE SNAKES!" Lee dove out of the bushes and into the red dirt.

This time Banjo crawled into the ferns and bushes

"ERRAMMMFF," went the dinosaur.

"Hee, hee, ha, haaa," laughed Banjo, who was now standing in a clearing. "Hey Lee, it's not a snake it's a baby Diplodocus. Take a look."

"A wha ...? Awww man, I thought it was a big snake. I HATE snakes!" Lee yelled as he crawled through the bushes and into the clearing. "Snakes should be outlawed."

Banjo was still laughing.

Dino was curiously watching the oversized baby wagging his fluffy tail. "Hey, it's a baby cow-dinosaur," he thought. "I don't think it will hurt us. He looks like a toy I had when I was a puppy, only this one is bigger ... a ... lot ... bigger."

It was the biggest baby anything the boys had ever seen. It was almost twenty feet long and it was mostly neck and tail. It was over seven feet tall at the highest part of its curved back.

The coloring was darker than an adult's, dark brown on top and rusty red on its underbelly. Its skin was thick, leathery and bumpy, sort of like elephant skin.

It was sniffing Lee now and shoving him with its nose. There were no dangerous smells on Lee, so the baby was not frightened.

"Hey, cut it out, you," scolded Lee. "What are you doing? I almost shot you, you know."

"Hee heee," laughed Banjo. "I think it likes you. It's checking you out."

"Hey, Banjo, look at this thing's face. It's weird," said Lee.

Banjo walked over carefully, so as not to scare the baby dinosaur. He was promptly sniffed and nudged by the baby. "Hey," laughed Banjo. He reached his hand out to touch the baby's face.

The baby lifted its head and let out an "ERRRRFF", then it let Banjo touch its face.

"Lips ... he has lips like a camel," said Banjo, as the baby tried to nibble his fingers. "Aaaah, easy on the fingers buddy," he said. "You can't eat them, you know. You're a plant-eater. It's against the rules."

"Ha haa," laughed Lee. "He may like me but he wants to eat you."

"Look," said Banjo, "his nostrils are almost on the tip of his nose. Some paleontologists thought they were on the top of their head, like a whale, but they are not."

"More paleontology theories bite the dust," said Lee.

The baby was now sniffing Dino. Dino whined and backed off at first, then cautiously sniffed the baby's face. The baby sniffed Dino and nibbled his fur with its camel-like lips. Dino was not sure about this. "I wonder what it tastes like?" he thought and licked the baby's face. "Hmmm, salty tasting," thought Dino. The baby liked that and licked Dino back with its long tongue. Its tongue was almost as long as Dino."MUMERUMPH," it said.

Dino jumped back and whined. "Whoa, easy with the monster tongue!" he thought. "You could tip over a car with that thing."

"Wow!" said Lee. "That tongue must be for grabbing branches and stuff. It's huge!"

"Yeah, I think the little guy is hungry. Let's get some tree branches and feed him," said Banjo.

"Good idea," said Lee. The boys began to pull branches down from a nearby tree to feed their hungry baby friend.

"Hey! Look how he eats," said Banjo, who was holding up a branch while the baby stripped all the leaves off of it with its long comb-like teeth. Banjo almost got pulled over trying to hold the branches. "This is so cool," he said. "I am actually feeding a Diplodocus."

Lee was not paying attention. He was staring at the sky with a worried look on his face. It was getting darker now. They were alone and Arbee was nowhere around. He had a feeling that the real nightmare was just beginning.

Chapter Eight
MEET DINKY DIPLODOCUS

Arbee landed the shuttle craft back aboard the starship and floated from the pilot's cabin to the back of the shuttle craft, where he thought the boys were.

"Well, well, that was another exciting day, was it not?" Arbee stopped. "Boys? Lee, Banjo, Dino, where are you?"

Just then Zinzu floated aboard. "Is something wrong?" he asked.

"Have you seen Dino and the boys? Did they get off the shuttle?" asked Arbee urgently.

"No, no one has left the shuttle," replied Zinzu.

"I do not understand. Banjo's locator coin showed up on my sensors ... wait," Arbee floated over to the bench where the boys had been seated. He looked under it and there he spotted a round shiny object on the floor. It was the locator coin he had given Banjo.

"GREAT FLAMING GALAXIES!" yelled Arbee. "They are still out there ALONE! Zinzu, we must find them, at once!"

"None of the ship sensors are working properly," said Zinzu unhappily. "What do you suggest we do?"

"We will have to go out to look for them ourselves," replied Arbee. "We have no time to worry about the sensors now. Put the starship on remote control and let us go and quickly!"

Arbee was horrified at the thought that his friends may have been hurt or killed in the Diplodocus stampede.

"I will set things up right away," replied Zinzu, as he flew out the door to make preparations for the search.

It was going to be a long night. With no shuttle or computers or sensors to assist them, they would have to search every inch of ground and forest to find Dino and the boys by themselves.

They had to find them fast, before the night predators did. That is, if they had not been trampled to death or eaten already.

"I wonder how this little guy got separated from his family?" asked Banjo, scratching the baby Diplodocus under its chin. The baby made sort of a purring sound and would not let Banjo stop.

Lee had been looking around the small clearing they were in. It was completely closed in by trees, vines and bushes except for a small opening.

"He must have crashed through here," said Lee, "and gotten stuck during the stampede. This clearing is like a corral or a cage. Man, I wish Arbee would get here. It's getting dark."

"We better build a fire," said Banjo.

"Okay, but make a small one," said Lee. "Arbee said dinosaurs are really scared of fire. That's just what we DON'T need is to stampede old what's-his-name over there," Lee added, pointing his thumb at the baby Diplodocus.

"Good idea," said Banjo. "Hey, what should we call this guy?"

"I don't know," answered Lee. "Why don't you name it? Wait ... is it a boy or a girl?"

"How should I know? Let's give it a name that could be either a he or a she," said Banjo. "How's about we call it Spudly?"

"Spudly ... seriously?" replied Lee. "That name is too stupid. We could name him after your bratty sister, Cassie."

"No way," laughed Banjo, "that would be an insult to the dinosaur community. I know, how about ... Monster Mutant Death Beast?"

"Cool name, but it's too long and too hard to remember," replied Lee, laughing. "And it doesn't fit. This guy looks more like a Bambi than a Monster Mutant ... whatever."

"Wait, wait, I know," interrupted Banjo. "What if we call him DINKY? I think Dinky is good."

The baby Diplodocus grunted, "Derrumph."

"See, he likes it!" said Banjo. "He likes the name."

"I think he just burped," said Lee. "But, what the heck, Dinky it is."

"Good," said Banjo with a smile. Then he spoke to the dinosaur. "Okay baby dinosaur, I hereby name you Dinky Diplodocus." Banjo patted the baby on the neck. Dinky responded by nibbling Banjo's bushy red hair.

"Ha, ha! He thinks you're a carrot, a big prehistoric carrot," laughed Lee. "Hey, I thought you were going to start a fire?"

"Yeah, yeah," said Banjo. "I am working on it."

Banjo went into his backpack and pulled out a container of waterproof camping matches and started a small fire on the side of the clearing and it did not seem to bother Dinky. Actually, Dinky was not even interested at all.

The boys took out some special "meal in a bar" granola bars and bottles of water and made a quick dinner.

"This sure isn't as good as my mom's meatloaf," commented Banjo.

SCOTT E. SUTTON

"It's better than nothing," replied Lee with his mouth full.

Banjo gave Dino a small packet of dog food and a couple of big dog biscuits.

Dinky snatched up one of Dino's dog biscuits, sloshed it around his mouth a few times and spit it out on the ground. "Errumff," dinky grunted. He was not happy with the dog biscuit at all.

Dino sniffed it but did not eat it. "Yuck, you slimed my dog biscuit. That one is yours now," he thought, "and quit eating my food. I don't go around eating your all your leaves and bushes."

"We should get some sleep," said Lee. "Who's going to stand watch?"

"Dino will," said Banjo. "Nothing can sneak up on him. He has got super dog senses."

Far off in the distance, in the moonlit prehistoric night the boys heard the trumpeting of the Diplodocus herd. Dinky let out a very sad moan.

"Dinky wants his mom," whispered Lee, staring up at the sky.

"Yeah, poor little guy," Banjo sighed. "You know, Lee, when Arbee comes, we have got to figure out how to get Dinky back to his herd. We can't just leave him here."

"I know," replied Lee. "We can't just leave him ... that would be bad especially with that pack of hungry Allosaurs running around."

The boys made pillows of their backpacks. Banjo put more wood on the fire, even though they really did not need it. The air was warm and comfortable. It was nice weather for such a dangerous place, but the fire might keep away any night hunting meat-eaters that might be sneaking around.

"Dino, guard!" commanded Banjo.

Dino lay down near the fire, facing the entrance to the clearing. He would sleep, but lightly, ready to defend the boys if he needed to. "It's going to be a long night," he thought.

Dinky let out a huge sigh and curled his long neck around so he could lay his head on his back. Then after crouching down to the ground, he closed his big brown eyes and slept, dreaming of being back with the herd and next to his mother where he belonged.

"Some paleontologists thought that Diplodocus and other long-necked plant-eaters didn't care for their young after they hatched. They said that they just left them in the bushes until they somehow grew up and joined a herd," said Banjo. "I guess they were wrong."

"There is no way baby plant-eaters could have survived in this place without protection from a herd," said Lee. "That makes no sense at all. Who is thinking up these theories?"

"We need to bring some paleontologists back with us to see what's really going on here," said Banjo.

Lee and Banjo lay on their backs and stared at the stars,

listening to the squawks, roars and calls of the nighttime dinosaurs and other creatures.

"Hey, Lee," said Banjo.

"What?" replied Lee.

"I don't recognize any of the constellations in the sky," replied Banjo.

"That's because this sky is a hundred and forty-six million years old," answered Lee. "The stars are in different places now."

"Oh yeah, I forgot that stars move around over time," said Banjo, yawning. He slowly drifted off into a deep sleep.

As worried as he was, Lee also fell asleep quickly too. It had been a long day and he was dead tired. Dinosaurs or no dinosaurs he could not keep his eyes open.

Everything was peaceful until nearly five hours later when Dino woke with a start. "That smell ... something's coming," he thought. "Grrrrrrr!" He let out a low warning growl. "Not this guy again. Don't these things ever sleep?"

Lee woke up, grabbed his slingshot and loaded it without thinking. He blinked his eyes to try and see what Dino was growling at.

"Hey ... Banjo, wake up," Lee whispered, shaking his friend. "Come on, get up."

"Huh, what?" Banjo woke up and grabbed his slingshot and loaded it, his eyes half open. "What's up?" he asked.

"Dino is growling at something over there," whispered Lee.

"Arbee, is that you?" said Banjo in a loud whisper.

"That is not Arbee," thought Dino, "not even close." "Grrrrr ... ruff," growled Dino.

Something big was breathing heavily at the entrance of the clearing and whatever it was had them trapped ... like rats in a trap.

Chapter Nine
DANGERS IN THE NIGHT

Zinzu and Arbee arrived at the last known location of Dino and the boys. They floated over the ground and began looking for some kind of tracks.

"What a mess," said Arbee. "The Diplodocus herd wiped out every trace of Dino and the boys."

"Not quite. Have a look here," said Zinzu. Arbee came over and Zinzu shined a light on the ground. There were some barely visible tennis shoe tracks. "It appears they fled that way, in the direction of the stampede."

"Good work," said Arbee. "At least we know they could very well be alive."

"Let us hope so," added Zinzu.

They followed the Diplodocus trail carefully searching the ground for clues.

"I have something else here," called Arbee.

Zinzu flew over. "It looks like some paw prints belonging to Dino," he said.

"There are not any dinosaurs that have foot prints like that. Let us keep searching around this area," said Arbee.

The search was going slowly. They had to search almost every inch of ground. At one point they went an entire hour without finding a single trace. Arbee had gone ahead to see if he could speed things up by picking up the boys' trail farther up the path.

"ZINZU," he called, after a long while, "OVER HERE, MORE TRACKS!"

Zinzu flew over.

"Here," pointed Arbee. There behind a large tree were the boys' and Dino's tracks.

"It appears they ran behind this tree for cover, but then ran off again in that direction," added Zinzu. "I do not understand why."

"Hmmm," replied Arbee. "Here is a possible reason. Look here, dinosaur tracks and some feathers. There were two meat-eaters here. They must have been hiding here before the boys and Dino arrived."

"Quickly, we must find the next closest tree. That was their plan of escape you see, to hide behind a tree for protection," explained Arbee. "That was a smart idea, I would say. Let us hope that it worked."

"It seems a sensible answer," replied Zinzu. The two aliens flew off into the night looking for the other tree.

The boys, Dino and Dinky were standing at the far side of the clearing, away from the entrance. Whatever the creature was that had awakened them still had not shown itself. Lee and Banjo had their slingshots ready.

The Diplodocus baby was getting very nervous, trying to back up into the solid wall of vines, plants and trees. He was whining silently.

There was a crackling of bushes, but still nothing showed itself. Then they saw the glimmer of two big yellow-green eyes about eight feet off the ground.

"What do you think it is?" asked Lee quietly.

"Bad news," replied Banjo. "Whatever it is, I am going to blast it before it charges."

"I hope you realize that if it is a meat-eater and we

shoot it, it's only going sleep for fifteen minutes," whispered Lee. "We are going to have to shoot it all night long."

Banjo sighed with disappointment. Lee was right. "We don't have much choice, do we?" he said, still aiming at the eyes in the dark. "It's either that or we get eaten."

The eyes lowered and slowly moved closer. There came a low growl and then a hissing. Dinky stayed very quiet and did not move, trying to blend in and not be seen.

All this time Dino was in a defensive stance, growling back. He knew what it was and that if it attacked he would have a tough fight ahead. "Oh well, that's a dog's life I suppose," he thought.

The creature crept silently into the clearing. With the glow from the flickering fire and the bright moonlight everyone was able to see the dinosaur's deadly features.

"Oh no, not him again," said Banjo. "It's that lousy Ceratosaurus, or one of his cousins."

"Wait, don't shoot," said Lee. "It's the fire that is keeping him back. I think that's why it hasn't charged, because of the fire. Cover me for a second, if I can scare it with fire ..."

"No way," interrupted Banjo. "If you do that you will be right in the way of my slingshot. I don't want to risk you getting hit because we don't know what these flash marbles do to people if they get zapped."

The dinosaur moved in closer, cautiously smelling the air. He was very uncertain about this. He remembered these

SCOTT E. SUTTON

creatures from before, something about a – FLASH – but he was hungry.

"He is going to charge," said Banjo. "We can't wait. Get ready. We shoot on three. One ... two ..."

But the boys did not get a chance to fire. From out of the sky came the ground-shaking call of a huge male Diplodocus, "EEEERRRRRRUMMMFF!"

The nervous Ceratosaurus had had enough, with the fire, the strange smells and now a fully grown Diplodocus. In an instant it turned and ran into the night to find an easier way to catch dinner. It was very tough being a meat-eater these days.

The boys looked around expecting to see the head and long neck of a big Diplodocus somewhere above them. Instead, slowly descending out of the sky they saw an unexpected but very welcome sight.

"Ah, ha, at last we have found you my friends. I must say, you had Zinzu and I very worried indeed!" said Arbee as he and Zinzu came floating into the clearing.

"ARBEE, YOU AND ZINZU FOUND US!" yelled Lee. "That's so cool!"

"YAHOO!" screamed Banjo, jumping up and down.

"Woooo woof!" barked Dino, also bouncing up and down. "I am so glad to see you guys." he thought. "I was not looking forward to fighting that big bird-lizard."

Dinky just stared at Arbee and Zinzu with a dumb,

confused look on his face. "Errumph," he grunted, as if to say, "You are not my mom. You're not even from my herd. What are you anyway?"

"I am terribly sorry that I left you behind," said Arbee. "But you dropped your locator coin on the shuttle craft, so naturally, I thought you were safely on aboard."

"I figured that out," said Lee. "But how come it took you so long to find us?" he added.

"There is a storm in space that is causing the electric energy around the planet to become unstable. It made our starship's computer sensors and electronics useless," Arbee replied. "Zinzu and I had to conduct the search ourselves. We had to look over every inch of ground for your foot prints, which I do not mind saying, was no easy task."

"I am just glad you found us," sighed Banjo. "I can't believe I lost the locator coin. That was pretty stupid."

"Do not say that Banjo," said Arbee. "You are not stupid. These things can happen to anyone. The good news is that you three figured out how to stay alive, and that was smart."

"Arbee, now that I know that everyone is safe, I need to go back to the starship to get the equipment working again," said Zinzu.

"Yes, go ahead and thank you for your help, Zinzu," replied Arbee. "I will be in contact later."

"Very well," said Zinzu, who flew up and disappeared into the night.

Dinky curled his long neck around and sniffed Arbee, then nudged him with his big head.

"Well, who do we have here? A new friend?" asked Arbee, scratching the baby under its chin, making Dinky purr.

"That's Dinky," replied Banjo. "We found him trapped here after the stampede and we are taking care of him."

"Dinky," said Arbee. "Hello, Dinky, nice to meet you." Arbee paused for a moment, looking at Dinky. "Hmmm, I think you should know something about our friend Dinky here. Dinky is a SHE not a HE."

"Oh," replied the boys.

"How do you know?" asked Lee.

"Trust me," answered Arbee. "Dinky is a she."

"Arbee, we have got to get Dinky back to the herd somehow," said Banjo. "I am not leaving her here to be eaten by some meat-eater. That Ceratosaurus is probably going to come back, or worse, that pack of Allosaurus."

"Yeah," agreed Lee. "We can't just leave her here. I would not want someone to do that to me."

"You are right I think, we cannot just leave her here," said Arbee, as he scratched Dinky under her chin. "That would be a most uncivilized thing to do."

The boys were relieved. They had not been sure what Arbee would think or if he would make them leave Dinky behind by herself.

"So, you can lift her up and fly her back to the Diplodocus herd, right?" asked Banjo, "with some kind of lift-beam or something?"

"My body works well but not that well," replied Arbee. "No, you see with the starship's sensors and all the electronics not working properly, we are going to have to walk our friend Dinky back to the herd … by ourselves … with no help from the shuttle craft, the starships or lift-beams."

"WHAT?" exclaimed the boys.

Chapter Ten
FOLLOW THE DUSTY RED ROAD

"WALK, you are kidding ... right?" yelled Lee. "Are you CRAZY?"

"I do not see any other way at this point," replied Arbee. "It is as I said ... the starship's electronics may not be working right for another ten hours or more. Besides, I can help protect you and, do not forget, you have the flash marbles I gave you to protect yourselves also. I think we will do just fine."

"It will be great!" exclaimed Banjo. "We have got weapons now."

"I knew you would say that," said Lee, shaking his head. "You guys are nuts. All right, when do we start?"

"The best time to start is right at sunrise, when the night predators are settling down to sleep and the day predators have not started hunting yet," explained Arbee. "That will give us a small window of time to get Dinky back to the herd."

"Sounds good," said Banjo cheerfully. "I am ready."

"NIGHT predators, DAY Predators, there are more PREDATORS than in a ZOO!" complained Lee. "We would be safer in a pit of alligators ... wearing pants made out of steak!"

"Cheer up," said Banjo. "We have got Arbee with us. And, it will be ... educational!"

"Banjo, here's some education for you. Do you want to know why all the mammals from this time period are no bigger than mice?" asked Lee, angrily.

"Why?" Banjo sighed, hoping Lee's lecture would end soon.

"Because all these PREDATORS eat EVERYTHING that MOVES!" screamed Lee.

"So, are you going with us or not?" asked Banjo.

"Yes," Lee grumbled.

"You boys might as well get some more sleep," said Arbee. "The sun will be rising in about four hours, so, I will stand guard for you."

"Are you going to sleep?" asked Lee.

"Oh no, my body does not need sleep," replied Arbee. "Do not worry, Lee. Get some rest. I can assure you that you will be safe."

So Dinky, Dino, Banjo and even Lee settled down into a deep sleep under the star-filled prehistoric sky while Arbee watched out for dinosaurs.

Four short hours later ...

"Lee, Lee ... it is time to wake up," whispered Arbee.

Lee woke up suddenly. He had been dreaming that he was playing chess with a talking Allosaurus who had very bad breath. "What time is it?" mumbled Lee, still half asleep and rubbing his eyes.

"Time to get up," laughed Banjo, munching something out of a small cup.

"It is almost dawn," said Arbee. "We must prepare to leave."

"Hey, Banjo, what are you eating? I am starved!" asked Lee. His mouth watering at the sight of food.

Arbee handed Lee a cup of some kind of cereal. "Eat this. It will give your body the fuel it needs. I formulated it myself with a food computer I have back on the starship. It's made from nuts, fruits and grains," he said.

"Eat it, Lee," mumbled Banjo, with his mouth full, "There isn't any milk to go with it but it's really good."

Lee took a spoonful and stuffed it into his mouth. "Mmmm, it is good. It tastes sweet and it's got nuts and berries and some kind of crunchy alien food stuff."

"Glad you like it," said Arbee, who was pleased with its

success. "Did you know that if a few changes in the human diet were made it could reduce diseases on your planet by more than half?" he asked.

"Mmmm," replied the boys, too busy gulping their food to listen. Dino was eating some of Arbee's dog biscuits for breakfast and Dinky had been busy chomping leaves for the past hour.

Between bites, Banjo noticed Dinky was eating but she was not chewing her food. She just stripped leaves off branches as fast as she could and swallowed.

"Hey, Arbee, how does a Diplodocus digest what they eat?" asked Banjo. "Dinky's not chewing her food."

"Dinky's not chewing her food because she, like the rest of her kind, does not have the back chewing teeth that you have," answered Arbee.

"Molars," said Lee, chomping away.

"Excuse me?" asked Arbee, a little confused.

"Molars," said Lee. "The back chewing teeth are called molars on this planet."

"Oh," said Arbee. "Yes, well, Dinky does not have molars. You see, these big plant-eaters have two stomachs. They scrape the leaves off the tree branches with their front teeth, the leaves then go into the first stomach. The leaves soften up in this first stomach and then go into a second stomach, called a gizzard."

"A gizzard is like a stomach that is lined with muscles

and is also lined with stones," explained Arbee. "When the stomach goes to work and flexes, the stones in the stomach act like teeth and grind up the food."

"How do the dinosaurs get stones into their gizzard?" asked Lee.

"They swallow them on purpose," interrupted Banjo. "Paleontologists find those gizzard stones inside the skeletons of plant-eating dinosaurs all the time. I've seen them in museums."

"Hmmm, isn't that how birds grind up their food," asked Lee, "with gizzards?"

"Correct," said Arbee, who floated over to Dinky and peeled back her big lip so the boys could see her teeth. Dinky didn't seem to mind. She just grunted.

"Wow," said Banjo, "those are weird teeth."

"They are like big pegs," added Lee, "and they could use a brushing, too. Dinky needs a dinosaur-dentist."

"Arbee, our scientists could never figure out where the Diplodocus had nostrils. They thought they were on top of their heads, but they aren't," said Banjo. "Do you know why?"

"No but when all you have is a pile of bones, sometimes just little pieces of bones, it is a wonder that your scientists could guess how any of these animals looked at all," explained Arbee. "I must say that from looking at your dinosaur books they have done a fairly good job on some dinosaurs and not so well on others."

"Well, that is enough of a science lesson for now," said Arbee, wiping the Diplodocus slobber off his hands. "Finish eating and let us 'hit the trail', as you say on Earth."

The boys gulped the rest of their cereal, put out the fire, then packed their gear into their backpacks. Banjo hooked Dino to his leash. "Okay," he said. "I am ready."

"BURP!" went Dino. "I am ready," he thought.

"Me, too," said Lee. "Hey, wait! How are we going to make Dinky follow us?"

"Leave that to me," replied Arbee.

Arbee made a strange grunting sound and almost immediately Dinky began to follow Arbee out of the protected clearing and onto the dusty red Diplodocus trail.

"Hey, that's great!" laughed Banjo. "We'll have to call you 'Arbee of the Jungle'!"

"Ha ha!" laughed Lee. "He can talk to the animals."

There was a chill in the air as the morning sky began to light up and the stars slowly faded away into blue.

"We will just follow the Diplodocus footprints until we reach the herd," said Arbee. "It is very simple."

"Well, how long do you think it will take?" asked Lee.

"Hmm ... I estimate about three hours," answered Arbee. "As long as the herd stays where it is and does not stampede again."

"Are you are saying three whole hours? This is not good. A lot can happen in three hours in this place," said Lee.

Banjo took a deep breath. He did not care how long it took. To him this was a great adventure. Then he remembered something, "Hey Dino, we have to get Dinky back to her herd as fast as we can so, don't stop to pee on EVERYTHING you sniff. Please?"

"Snort" went Dino. "You're no fun at all. Besides peeing on bushes is how dogs figure out where we are. It's like 'dog-global-positioning'."

Arbee laughed when he heard Dino's thought.

"What's so funny?" asked Lee.

"Oh nothing," said Arbee. "It was something Dino just thought."

Arbee and the Science Team made good time with Dinky hiking down the long, dusty trail.

"I don't think Dinky likes being out in the open," Banjo noticed. Dinky had been moving quickly and the boys had to walk fast just to keep up her.

"That's because she knows she is a sitting duck out here for Allosaurs or other meat-eaters that want to make her into a Diplodocus burger for lunch," said Lee.

"She wants to get back to her herd," said Arbee. "This is no place for a baby Diplodocus to be, without the protection of her herd."

"Don't worry, Dinky. We'll get you home," said Banjo, patting her on her side, making a cloud of dust. "Cough, cough ... You need a bath, Dinky!" he laughed. "We'll have to call you Stinky Dinky."

"Now you need a bath, too," laughed Lee. "Stinky Banjo!"

"Ha! You should talk," thought Dino. "People all smell funny to me."

Arbee laughed again at Dino's thought.

"What's so funny, now?" asked Lee.

"Oh, nothing," sighed Arbee. "It is just something else Dino thought. He is quite funny you know."

"I still can't get used to you talking to Dino," mumbled Banjo. "It freaks me out."

As they walked on, Lee picked up some stones and was tossing them here and there into the bushes on the side of the trail when one of the stones he threw went – THUD. Lee had accidentally hit something. "WHOOP, WHOOP, WHOOP!" came strange calls as a number of very upset dinosaurs leaped from the underbrush like kangaroos.

"YIKES!" yelled Lee, as both boys grabbed their slingshots and loaded them with flash marbles.

Dino barked at the creatures, "ARF, ARF, ARF, Grrrrr."

"Easy, easy," interrupted Arbee. "They are plant-eaters, there is no need to shoot them. They are harmless."

SCOTT E. SUTTON

“Phew! Okay,” said Lee, nervously. “Plant-eaters ... that’s good.”

“Wow, look at them,” said Banjo. “What are they?” he asked. He grabbed his computer out of a pocket on his backpack and scanned through the dinosaur computer book. “Let’s see ... hmmm.”

The creatures were standing there looking at the strangers. They saw the baby Diplodocus and realized there was no threat and even though Dino was barking at them the dinosaurs did not seem to be bothered. They went back to nipping off branches with their beaked mouths.

“I believe they are Dryosaurs,” said Arbee, “a common plant-eater from this time period.”

“Yep, you’re right., Here’s a picture of one right here,” said Banjo.

Lee looked at it. “The drawings look sort of close, except for the color,” he said, looking back at the creatures.

The Dryosaurus was about as tall as a fully grown man and they stood on two legs, had long arms and hands. They also had beaks for cutting and biting off leaves of plants and trees to eat. Their body coloring was similar to a zebra, except the stripes were a very pale yellow green and a faded dark green instead of black and white. The dinosaurs moved off quietly, to get away from Dino’s annoying barking.

“Let’s chase these things,” he was thinking, straining at his leash. “They can’t hurt us. Come on, please?”

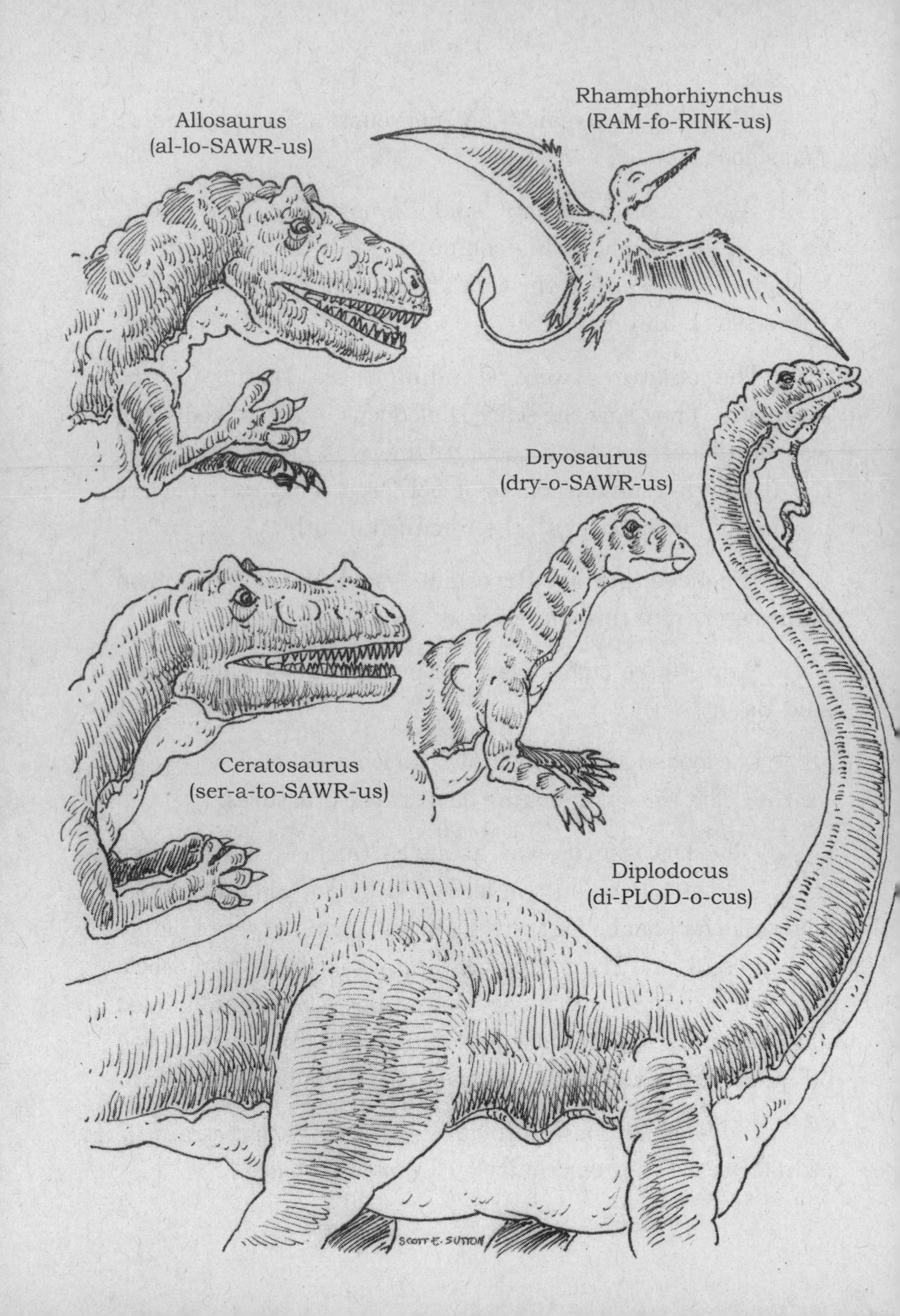
Rhamphorhiynchus
(RAM-fo-RINK-us)
Allosaurus
(al-lo-SAWR-us)
Dryosaurus
(dry-o-SAWR-us)
Ceratosaurus
(ser-a-to-SAWR-us)
Diplodocus
(di-PLOD-o-cus)
SCOTT E. SUTTON

"Sorry, Dino, we must keep moving," said Arbee. "And, Lee, no more rock throwing, please."

"Okay," said Lee. "Sorry about that, I didn't think I would actually hit anything."

"Just be glad you didn't hit an Allosaur," said Banjo.

The sun had risen higher into the sky by now and the day was alive with the chirps, squawks and growls of insects, dinosaurs, and other prehistoric creatures.

"Phew, it's starting to get real hot," said Lee.

After a long distance the dusty Diplodocus trail finally led them to a slow moving river. The water looked cool, clear and inviting.

"Is this water safe to drink, Arbee?" asked Banjo.

"I would not advise it," he replied. "Drink from your bottles. However, you can splash some on your hands and face to cool off. But do not get any in your mouth or eyes. There could be germs in the water that might make you sick."

"Okay," said Banjo, as he ran toward the river.

When Banjo was nearly to the river's edge he tripped over something on the ground that made him fall to his knees in the red dirt and mud.

"Nice, dude," laughed Lee. "Did you have a nice trip?"

Banjo stood up looking down at the ground where he had just fallen. "Hey Arbee, you better come have a look at these ... they look really fresh."

Chapter Eleven

THE BATTLE OF ALLOSAURUS ALLEY

"What is it?" asked Lee.

"Dinosaur tracks," said Banjo, "and they were definitely made by meat-eaters. Rats, we just can't get away from those things, can we?"

"Yes, I see," said Arbee, looking at the ground. "Those are Allosaurus tracks alright." Arbee floated over the spot by the river where the footprints were. "There are quite lot of them, too," he said.

Arbee counted to himself the number of tracks in the red mud. "It looks like there are at least eight or nine individual Allosaurs, possibly more. These tracks are fresh, as you said, Banjo. I was hoping we would avoid these fellows," said Arbee.

Dino whined when he smelled the Allosaurus prints. "Oh, not these guys again," he thought. "There are bird-lizards around here, they are close and there are lots of them."

"These tracks must belong to the Allosaurs we saw chasing the Diplodocus herd," said Banjo. "They are the ones that caused the stampede, I will bet you."

"Great! How are we going to get Dinky past nine Allosaurs?" asked Lee.

"Well, let me call the ship," said Arbee, pushing a button on his chest. "This is Arbee to Zinzu. Come in please."

"Zinzu here," the assistant replied. His voice could barely be heard.

"What is the current situation with the storm?" asked Arbee.

"The planets electronic storm is continuing longer than I predicted and it will continue for at least six more hours," answered Zinzu.

"Hmmm, not good," said Arbee. "Alright Zinzu, keep me informed of any changes in the storm, Arbee out."

"I will let you know as soon as there is any change, Zinzu out."

"Well, Banjo, Lee and Dino," said Arbee, "it appears that we are completely on our own. If we want to get Dinky home to the herd then you two had better load your slingshots and stick close to me. Dino, I hope those teeth of yours are sharp because we might need them today so stay close. We are going to have to fight this pack of prehistoric wolves ourselves, as best we can."

"Walking around here with Dinky is like walking through a lion's cage with a necklace of hot dogs around your neck," said Lee

"I don't care, we are not leaving Dinky here alone!" said Banjo in an angry voice.

"Of course NOT," Lee yelled back. "I didn't SAY that!"

"Okay," said Banjo, loading his slingshot. "Red alert."

"Okay," grumbled Lee. "Red alert." He also loaded his sling shot. "Make sure you have plenty of flash marbles where you can get at them. We don't want to run out of marbles just as some Allosaur is trying to eat us."

"Good idea," replied Banjo. He put his marbles into an easier to get to pocket. "Okay, I am good."

"All right, boys," said Arbee. "We need a plan of action. First, we must move quickly and quietly. Second, we must keep close to the river so we only have one side to protect. The Allosaurs will not attack from the other side of the river because it is too open."

"What about using Dino as our early-warning system?" said Banjo. "He can smell a meat-eater a mile away. I can let him off his leash so he can move around and spot for us."

"Excellent idea," said Arbee, "as long as he does not run off."

Banjo took Dino's leash off and spoke to him, "Listen Dino, you stay close and let us know where those big bird-lizard things are. You got it?"

Dino licked Banjo on his face. "Got it, but if I kill one of those giant bird-lizard things then you have got to cook it for me and let me eat it."

Arbee went over the rest of his plan to everyone. "Banjo, you and Lee stay close to Dinky on her left side, with your slingshots loaded and ready. I will fly out front and stop any Allosaurs that try to attack us before they get to Dinky. Dino, you must run in front of Dinky and behind me. Let me know when you smell anything coming. Now, are there any questions?"

"Nope," replied Banjo.

"I am as ready as I will ever be," said Lee, "so let's get this over with. If my mom ever knew what I was doing she would totally freak out."

"WOOF!" barked Dino. "Finally, I will get to go after some of those stupid bird-lizards instead of them chasing me all of the time," he thought. "Let's go."

"Good," said Arbee, "off we go and as you say ... stay on red alert!"

They started off again, staying close to the rushing river. The boys wished they could jump into the clear water and cool off, but there was no time for that now.

They entered a dense forest of giant redwood trees where the river flowed. It covered the trail like a thick green umbrella. They moved on with caution, looking carefully into the underbrush. Off in the distance they heard the calls of

the Diplodocus herd.

“Good, we are getting closer,” whispered Banjo.

“EEEERRUMF,” Dinky was trying to send a call to her mother.

Lee whapped Dinky on her side to get her attention, “Shhhh, Dinky, be quiet,” Lee said in a loud whisper. “You will have every Allosaurus in the world over here!”

The path along the river curved further into the forest. It was cooler and darker now because the trees were blocking the hot sunlight but still, everybody was very tense. This was a perfect place for an Allosaur or a pack of Allosaurs to attack them.

Just a few minutes later Dino stopped. His tail and ears went down and he let out a low growl. “Here they come, it’s the big bird-lizards,” he thought. “Get ready!”

“GRRRRAAA!” a huge Allosaurus leaped out of the bushes to the left and behind the boys. It charged.

The beast was fast, but Banjo was faster – THWACK – He fired and – SWOOSH, FLASH … THUD – Down came Allosaurus number one. Banjo reloaded.

“Nice shot, Banjo,” said Lee, nervously. “Oh, man! This is nuts … totally nuts!”

Dinky had a horrified look in her eyes. The sight of the knocked out Allosaurus lying on the path made her panic.

“ERRRREEEE!” she screamed and started running

down the path along the river's edge in the direction of the Diplodocus herd. She thought getting back to her parents was her only chance of survival.

"She is running away!" screamed Lee.

"Keep up with her!" called Arbee, who was still out in front. "Watch the left side. They will attack from the forest. The Allosaurs will go for Dinky, not for you."

The boys ran to stay alongside of Dinky. Their slingshot pouches were loaded and pulled back, ready to shoot.

Dino, running in front of Dinky, barked a warning, "Arf, arf, arf."

CRASH – Another Allosaurus jumped out to block Dinky's retreat. ZAP – Arbee was there in an instant, shooting a bolt of blue light from his arm. Allosaurus number two was thrown back and fell into the dust.

Dinky kept running forward, but she was panicking and her calls were attracting attention. She ran into the river to get around the body of the fallen Allosaurus. From the tree line everyone heard strange calls coming from the forest, "ERK ... ERK ... ERRRK!" as if the Allosaurs were alerting each other and planning an attack.

"The Allosaurs know we are here," said Arbee. "Stay close together. Watch your left. They will attack from the left!"

"I am going to try something!" yelled Banjo. – THWACK – Banjo fired his slingshot into the part of the forest where he

SCOTT E. SUTTON

had heard Allosaurs' calls and – FLASH – Allosaurs number three and number four fell from their hiding place behind a large tree.

"Good shooting, Banjo!" yelled Arbee. "Stay together now and keep MOVING!"

"ERK ... ERK ... ERRRK ..." more Allosaur attack calls were coming from all over the forest.

THWACK, THWACK – Lee and Banjo fired into the direction of the sounds but ... nothing.

"Nuts!" yelled Lee. "I MISSED!"

"RELOAD!" yelled Banjo. "RELOAD!"

"GRRAAHH!" A smaller Allosaurus leaped from some nearby bushes onto the path and charged Dinky.

The boys' slingshots were not loaded and Arbee was too far ahead to help Dinky. Dino growled and prepared to fight. "Come on you stupid lizard!" he thought. "I am going to make dog food out of you!" But before Dino could attack ...

"ERRUMMFF!" Dinky screamed in anger and charged at the small Allosaurus. The boys were shocked.

"What was Dinky doing?" Said Banjo

"Lee and Banjo, GET DOWN!" screamed Arbee. "GET DOWN ON THE GROUND NOW!"

The boys dove into the dirt and good thing they did.

Dinky stopped short of the oncoming Allosaurus and

swung her long tail around like a giant whip right over Lee's and Banjo's head. It came as fast as a rocket – SWOOSH, WHAM – the unlucky Allosaurus number five flew head over heels and – CRACK – into a nearby tree then – THUD – onto the ground. Its neck was broken and blood gushed from its open, tooth-lined mouth. Its days of hunting were over.

"Whoa, did you see THAT?" said Lee. "This baby Diplodocus is DANGEROUS!"

"No wonder Diplodocus grow so big! They are tough," said Banjo, who finally got his slingshot loaded.

Dino was starring at Dinky amazed at what she had done. But then he smelled that smell again, turned towards the forest and sounded the alarm, "Arf, arf, arf, arf."

"There is one OVER THERE!" yelled Banjo.

Lee shot and – FLASH – down went Allosaurus number six. "HAH ... sweet dreams!" said Lee. He was starting to feel confident. They just might get out of this mess after all. "I hope we get to the herd soon," he thought. "The flash marbles I have will not last forever."

Arbee, Dino, the boys and Dinky were coming to the end of the forest. Beyond its edge they saw a welcome sight.

"The Diplodocus herd is straight ahead!" yelled Arbee. "We are almost there, keep moving."

"GRRRRAH," there was a cry from the woods as still another meat-eater ran towards them – THWACK, SWOOSH, THUMP – Banjo had downed Allosaurus number seven before it could even leave the tree line.

Lee and Banjo were breathing hard and were soaked with sweat. Even in the shade of the forest the heat was intense.

At the edge of the forest Arbee waited for the others to catch up. He floated next to a tree. "This way," he yelled, "this way, we are almost ..."

Arbee never saw the huge meat-eater run at him, from behind, until it grabbed him by his arm.

"LOOK OUT ... ARBEE!" the boys yelled. But it was too late. The biggest Allosaurus they had ever seen had just grabbed Arbee by the arm with its powerful jaws and was about to tear him to pieces!

Chapter Twelve

DON'T MESS WITH DINOSAUR DOG

"IIIEEE!" screamed Arbee, as the huge Allosaurus swung him around by his arm like a helpless rag doll.

"Oh, no, ARBEE!" yelled Banjo.

"What are we supposed to do now?" yelled Lee. "If we shoot the flash marbles we will knock out Arbee. Or will we?"

"Heck if I know," answered Banjo in a panic. "I forgot to ask! Oh man, this is BAD! I don't know what to do!"

Dino, seeing the situation Arbee was in, leaped into action. He wasted no time and charged in like a furry missile aimed directly at the giant meat-eater to try to save his friend, Arbee."

"Oh no, oh no! DINO, GET BACK HERE!" yelled Banjo. He pulled his slingshot back, ready to shoot.

"NO!" yelled Lee. "Don't shoot, you might hit Arbee!"

"Tough beans," Banjo screamed back. "If that Allosaurus grabs my dog, he is so dead, I don't care, I will BLAST it, I swear to you ... I WILL!"

Dinky and the boys had stopped moving forward. They were right at the edge of the forest now. Banjo and Lee were aiming and waiting to see what happened next and ready to shoot if they needed to, while at the same time, they were watching the forest to their left for another Allosaurus sneak attack.

They were shaking with fear and excitement. Sweat was pouring down their faces, stinging their eyes so badly they had a hard time seeing.

"GRRRR, ARF, ARF, ARF!" Dino barked like a mad dog as he swiftly got closer and closer to the huge dinosaur.

When he got to the Allosaurus he did something that no one expected. He leaped up and bit the dinosaur on its underbelly, sinking his large Chow Chow teeth into its skin and held on tight, shaking his head violently. The dinosaur's skin was thick and tough, but Dino would not let go.

"Stinking pesky bird-lizard!" he thought. "I'll teach you! GRRR! Welcome to dog city!"

The confused Allosaurus roared and released Arbee from its grip. Arbee floated away to safety holding on to his damaged arm.

Dino let go of the monster's belly and quickly scurried

under its feet and bit it on the back of its leg, growling wildly. The Allosaurus trying to bite and kick Dino off its leg, lost its balance and fell over – WHAM – onto its side, raising a huge explosion of red dust, rocks and dirt!

"Yeah, DINO!" yelled Banjo, still aiming his weapon at the downed dinosaur. "Now get OUT OF THERE."

Arbee let out a loud whistle. "Dino come here boy, come on Dino, you got him good! It is time to go!"

Dino released the Allosaurus from his bite and ran away from the dinosaur toward Banjo. A smart Chow Chow knows when to fight and when to run, and now was a good time to run.

Lee and Banjo were waiting for a clear shot, saw their chance and fired – FLASH, FLASH – They knocked out Allosaurus number eight.

"Hah, you stupid bird-lizard!" thought Dino. "I taught you. Hey, did I kill it? I think I killed it! Remember, someone needs to cook that thing up for me for dinner. I will bet you it tastes like chicken."

"Lee, Banjo and Dino," yelled Arbee, "come along now, our job is not done yet, hurry!"

The Diplodocus herd was becoming very interested in what was happening at the edge of the forest. Some of the bigger ones were coming closer to investigate, having heard Dinky's call for help.

Dinky and the boys were running into the clearing

SCOTT E. SUTTON

now. Arbee came back to join them.

"Arbee are you okay?" yelled Lee.

"My arm is damaged, but it is nothing serious. I will be fine," he answered. "Now, we must keep moving!"

"ERRRUMMF!" called Dinky to the herd.

"EEERRRUMMMMF!" Several calls came back from the herd. A number of huge Diplodocus were now running to Dinky's aid.

Banjo glanced back toward the forest. "Lee, there are two ... no ... three Allosaurs coming after us!" he yelled.

"Arbee," yelled Lee, "make sure Dinky gets to the herd."

"Right, I am on my way," Arbee called back. Arbee made some sort of Diplodocus call that made Dinky run faster.

Dinky was now running as fast as she could, her tail flying in the wind. She was desperately calling out loudly to her family as she ran.

The Allosaurs were getting closer fast. The boys each knew what each other was thinking. They stopped, turned, took aim and fired – THWACK, THWACK, SWOOSH – It was a long shot, but – FLASH, FLASH – two of the three Allosaurs dropped into the dust and ferns.

The third Allosaurus tripped over the body of one of its fallen companions and went head first into a bunch of tall ferns, "GRRRRAAAA!" it screamed with pain.

"Dinky made it back," yelled Lee, as he saw Dinky run

back into the protection of the herd and her mother. "Finally, she made it."

"Yeah, well, that's great ... but ... we have got bigger problems over here," said Banjo, reloading. "Look what's coming!"

"Aw nuts," said Lee, as he saw two more Allosaurs coming straight for them, and three more at the edge of the forest. "How many of these stupid things are there?"

"Too many," yelled Banjo. "Just hurry up and reload, quick. This is not over yet!"

The boys prepared to fire but were interrupted by Arbee's voice. "Forget the Allosaurs, boys!" he yelled. "We have had enough of battling with them today. It is time that we leave! Dinky is safe at home now. Hang on!"

WHOOSH! Arbee scooped Banjo and Lee up off the ground and into the air.

"Wait, where's DINO?" screamed Banjo. "My dog DINO ... where ..."

"I have him. I have him," said Arbee. "Do not worry, he is quite safe!"

"Arf, arf, arf," Dino barked at the Allosaurs. "Hah, bird-lizards," he thought. "Do you know why you bird-lizards went extinct? It's because DOGS finally showed up, that's why."

Arbee had taken Lee, Banjo and Dino off the ground just in time because a few seconds later a Diplodocus, who was one hundred feet long, ran out and swung his monstrous tail into action – SWOOSH!

The two charging Allosaurs had stopped and turned to flee the angry dinosaur. But – THWAP – it was too late for one of them, who was knocked all the way back to the tree line and broke its back on a tree dying instantly. The other

one barely managed to escape back into the forest.

"ERRRRUMMMFF!" The mighty Diplodocus, along with a number of others in the herd, let out horrifying warning cries and stood up on their hind legs. Their gigantic bodies seemed to fill the entire sky.

The remaining Allosaurs, seeing the battle was lost, retreated, one by one back into the cover of the forest. These were tough times to be a meat-eater.

The Diplodocus was not a dinosaur to be taken lightly. The huge, muscular dinosaurs came back down onto four legs with an earth shaking – BOOM. They stood for a moment and let out more loud warning calls. Then, seeing the Allosaurs retreat to the forest, they wandered slowly back to rejoin the rest of the herd.

"Whoa, that was so awesome!" gasped Banjo.

"Holy cows," whispered Lee. "I've never seen anything like that!"

Paleontologists had wondered how plant-eaters such as the Diplodocus had survived long enough to grow so huge. The boys could now see why. The Diplodocus herd was like a large family, working together fiercely protecting their young, much like the elephants of present-day Earth. They did not always succeed but they succeeded enough to live a very long time.

Arbee flew over the herd and the boys yelled a farewell to Dinky.

Dinky looked up and let out one last "EERUMF!" Her mother was licking her as if to clean her up.

"Good!" laughed Banjo. "She needs a bath!"

"Yuck, Diplodocus spit! Dinky is getting a spit bath," said Lee.

Arbee flew back to the starship so they all could get themselves cleaned up as well.

After a "light" shower, the boys and Dino sat down to a big meal prepared by "Chef Arbee". They were hungry and tired.

"I don't know what this is," mumbled Banjo, "but it's great. Tastes like chicken."

“Hey,” said Lee. “This isn’t Martian sea slugs or some other weird alien food is it? I don’t want to grow an arm out my head, you know. I have to go to school on Monday.”

“Nonsense!” laughed Arbee. “Eat up, now. Martian sea slugs, indeed! You Earth people have the wildest imaginations.”

“Hey, Arbee how’s your arm?” asked Banjo, still busy eating. “Can you fix it or do you have to go to a robot hospital or something?”

“All fixed, you see?” Arbee showed them his new arm, flexing his fingers. “I must say, you boys did a brave thing out there today saving Dinky like that. And Dino, well, what can I say? You were very brave, indeed.”

“Dogs are naturally brave,” thought Dino, “even little ones. But the little ones are kind of crazy, so be careful.”

“More crazy than brave,” said Lee.

“Burrrp,” belched Banjo. “We couldn’t have pulled it off without you, Arbee.”

“Hey, mind your manners, slob!” laughed Lee, nudging Banjo.

“Well, excuse me!” said Banjo. “What are you, the burp police?”

“Yes, well, advanced science is very helpful,” Arbee said, moving his new arm again. He was glad he did not have a flesh body like the boys. “They are so much harder to repair,” he thought.

Dino stretched, yawned and went back to his nap. He was dreaming of chasing rabbits – nice, cute, furry, little rabbits that were not thirty feet long and did not have six-inch-long teeth.

After a short rest, Arbee took Dino and the boys out one more time in the shuttle craft to explore.

The storm that had caused his sensors and electronics to not work had passed. They watched the Diplodocus herd, and even saw Dinky again. They were all in a lake drinking huge amounts of water, taking a bath and eating plants.

"She looks happy to be home," said Lee.

"She looks clean, too," laughed Banjo. "No more stinky Dinky."

"Speaking of home," mentioned Arbee, "I believe it is time we all do the same. I have to get back to Planet Izikzah and catalog all our research for the central library."

He flew the shuttle craft back to the starship and escorted Dino and the boys to the time tunnel entrance after they had said goodbye to Zinzu.

"Turn in your slingshot flash marbles until next time," ordered Arbee. The boys handed the remaining silver marbles to Arbee. Banjo would have liked to keep a few, but he did not.

"We are all set then," he said. "I will see you in two weeks?"

"Yeah, that would be great!" said Banjo.

“How are you going to find us?” asked Lee. “Banjo lost the locator coin you gave him, remember?”

“Oh, yes!” said Arbee. “I almost forgot. Wait here for a moment.” Arbee went back into the starship briefly and returned. “I made something that will not be so easy to lose.” Arbee handed both Lee and Banjo a stretchy cloth wristband made of the same camouflage cloth as their clothing.

“Cool!” said Banjo, who slipped his on. “I won’t lose this.”

“Yes. The locator coin is sewn right into the wristband. And, look, I made a collar for Dino, too.” Arbee explained. “Now you all, hopefully, will not be getting lost again.”

“Yeah, that was scary,” said Lee, “but what happens if, like, the FBI or the Air Force gets hold of these? It’s alien science stuff. If they find out we’ll be in big trouble.”

“If they get hold of it, they would find what looks like a useless piece of metal sewn into an even more useless piece of cloth and they would throw it away,” answered Arbee. “I do not mean to offend you, but I am not about to hand over any advanced science to your planetary authorities, they are dangerous enough as it is.”

“Yeah, I see, you don’t want them to use it to blow stuff up, right?” said Lee. “Well, we better go. We’ll be seeing you Arbee and thanks for everything!”

“Woof!” said Dino, wagging his tail. “Life is a lot more fun around here,” he thought. “And thanks for the biscuits.”

Arbee gave him a pat on the head. "Yes, see you next time, Dino," he said, "and do try to stay out of trouble."

"Bye, Arbee," said Banjo. "See you in two weeks!"

"Two weeks it is," replied Arbee.

FLASH – Dino and the boys were gone, into the time tunnel and back to the safety of their world… back to the age of humans.

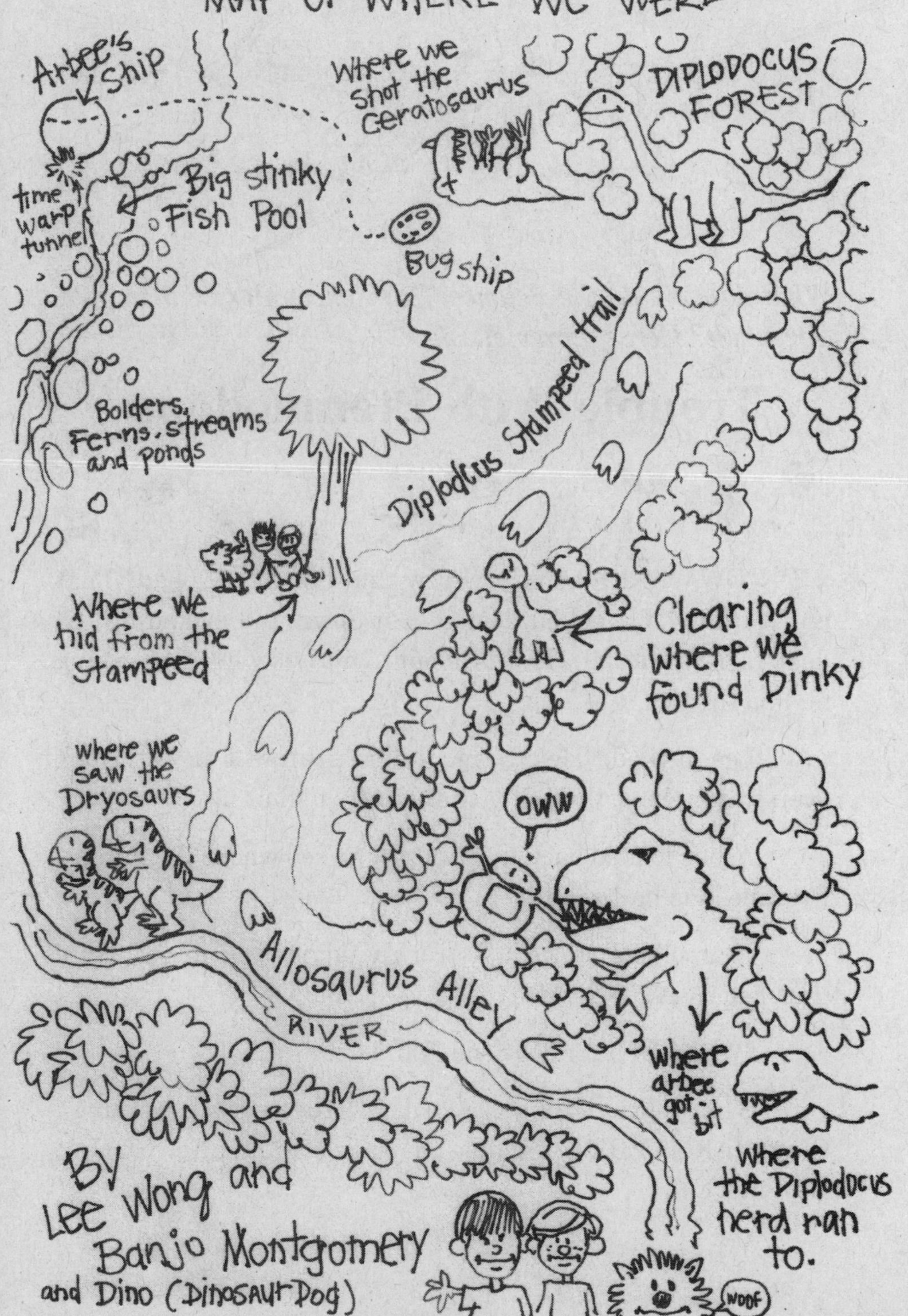
MAP OF WHERE WE WERE
Arbee's Ship
time warp tunnel
Big stinky Fish Pool
Where we shot the Ceratosaurus
Bug ship
DIPLODOCUS FOREST
Bolders, Ferns, streams and ponds
Diplodcus Stampeed trail
Where we hid from the Stampeed
Clearing where we found Dinky
where we saw the Dryosaurs
OWW
Allosaurus Alley
RIVER
where arbee got bit
Where the Diplodocus herd ran to.
By Lee Wong and Banjo Montgomery
and Dino (Dinosaur Dog)
WOOF

What dangers do the Science Team encounter in their next adventure? Here's a preview of:

Trouble With Pteranodons

"OWW! Alright, who threw that fish at my head? That is not funny!" he yelled. Banjo bent down and picked up the dead fish by the tail. He was about to hit Lee with it, thinking he had thrown it at him.

Lee ducked. "Hey, Banjo, I didn't throw it at you. Don't even think about throwing that stinky fish at me!"

Arbee looked back into the sky to see where the hungry Pteranodons had gone.

"Banjo!" he yelled. "I strongly advise you to get rid of that fish ... AT ONCE!"

"What? What about the fish?" said Banjo.

Sam yelled, "Banjo, do what Arbee says ... drop ... the ... fish and RUN because they are coming after YOU ... HURRY UP!"